Bombay Bhel

stories by
Ken Doyle

 Loquent

Loquent Press
Fitchburg, Wisconsin, USA

Published by Loquent Press, a division of Loquent LLC
Fitchburg, Wisconsin, USA
www.loquent.net/press

ISBN-10: 061576357X
ISBN-13: 978-0615763576 (Loquent Press)

First edition February 2013

Original cover photograph by Christian Haugen
www.christianhaugen.com

Cover and book design by Loquent Press

Printed in the United States of America

for my parents

Contents

Aam Papad

THE TRAIN WHEEZED in relief as it slowed to a crawl and then came to a dead stop. Hassan leaned against the rust-tinged bars of the window, coughing as the cloying stench of sewage from the Thana creek filled his lungs. In the distance, he could see the oncoming train growing larger as it hurtled along the curve of the adjacent track. As it flew past, the welcome rush of air helped clear his head better than the ineffectual drone of the overhead fans, trapped in their steel cages. He mopped his face with a stained cloth, sat back in the unyielding wooden bench seat, and closed his eyes.

He'd left as soon as he'd heard the news that morning from one of his neighbors, who charged up four flights of stairs to deliver it. A few panicked words, between gasps for air, convinced Hassan that he had no time to waste. The usual assortment of snack foods for his day's sales lay in a heap on his kitchen table. His neighbor promised to take care of everything as Hassan handed him the keys to the flat. Hassan had the forethought to stuff a handful of food into the ample pockets of his loose-fitting kurta before running out the door.

He flagged down a taxi as he left the building. The driver,
upon hearing Hassan's plight, put a little extra effort into
weaving his way through the impenetrable mass of morning
traffic before depositing him at Bombay Central station. Hassan
joined the meandering line at the counter and purchased a
ticket for the next train to Kapilgaon. After a half-hour wait,
he found himself on the Bhusawal Passenger, a daily service
that required no reservations. Fortunately, it wasn't bursting at
the seams like the yellow and brown local trains traveling in the
opposite direction. They arrived every few minutes, vomiting
great streams of humanity that split into two as they left the
station: one headed towards Tardeo Circle and connecting
buses, the other eventually dispersed into Bombay's southern
core. As Hassan had walked through the cabin, stepping over
baskets of vegetables and an old steamer trunk, he'd found a
window seat without much difficulty.

Now, as the train began moving again, Hassan heard a few
passengers discussing the riots in Kapilgaon. The news was
still making its way to Bombay, but it hadn't taken long. As he
began to sway to the four-beat rhythm of the train's wheels, his
stomach reminded him that he hadn't eaten as yet.

He fumbled in his pockets and emerged with an irregular,
leathery sheet of aam papad. The tangy sweetness of the
dried mango pulp flooded his mouth, uncut by the customary
seasoning of rock salt and chili powder. He closed his eyes
again, chewing with a determined concentration as he leaned
his head against the thin laminate of the compartment wall,
worn smooth with the grease and sweat of thousands of
heads each day. He thought of the boy who was a regular
visitor outside the school gates, the one who always ordered

aam papad. He wondered if he would realize where Hassan had gone.

Brian looked at the clock on the wall, perfectly centered below the faded crucifix. He shifted in his seat and tried to refocus his gaze on the blackboard as his Marathi teacher delivered a monologue about pluperfect tenses and possessive pronouns.

Brian had developed a strong dislike for Marathi classes ever since the second standard, when his teacher had commented on the odd way he pronounced certain words. Like all the other makapaos, she said. At the time, he had no idea what she meant, but he later learned that a makapao was a Goan Catholic and soon began to use the term himself, taking pride in wearing the label. He learned other labels, too. Parsis were bawas, Gujaratis were gujjus, Mangaloreans were mangies, and he, Brian Alphonso Fernandes, was a makapao.

The red hand on the clock continued its relentless sweep around the stark white face. For a moment, the hands froze in perfect alignment, pointing to the twisted body on the cross. Yet the bell refused to ring. As often happened, the bell-ringer's clock at St. Magnus didn't agree with the one in Brian's fifth-standard, division A classroom. He drummed his fingers on the desktop as he glanced at the maze of ink-stained graffiti carved into its surface. The teacher frowned at him, pausing in mid-sentence. Brian caught her stare out of the corner of his eye and looked away at once, pretending to be absorbed in his notebook. The empty silence seemed to stretch on forever. At last, the teacher resumed her lesson.

The bell buzzed like a swarm of bees trapped in a tiffin box, and the class rose as one in a symphony of chairs scraping the polished concrete floor. Brian stuffed his books into the worn backpack that lay at his feet. He waited for the teacher to wrap up the lesson and joined half-heartedly in the chorus as the boys chanted, "*Aamhi abhari ahot, bai,*" thanking her and wishing her a good day. He sprinted through the classroom door. The backpack slapped his side as it dangled from one shoulder.

A chain at the top of the main school gates held them open just wide enough to let the usual procession of tiffin carriers trickle through. Brian knew a few of his classmates whose families were privileged enough to afford the service, occasionally envying them the special delivery of home-cooked meals. He, like most of the students at St. Magnus, made do with the standard fare at the school canteen. The food vendors who camped outside the gates provided a welcome diversion from the canteen's bland and predictable menu, and they were Brian's first stop during the lunch hour. He walked through the gates and frowned as he tried to peer over the heads of the crowd gathered on the pavement. There was no sign of Hassan for the third day that week. In place of the familiar aluminum tray perched on a wicker stand, a void yawned at him like a tear in the fabric of the universe itself.

Brian continued through the press of bodies and headed further up the street, toward the bridge that curved over the adjacent railway tracks. Maybe Hassan had simply taken a different spot, perhaps outside the smaller gates that led into the junior school playground. But the only vendor there was the golawala, in his usual location. Brian watched as he cranked the bright red wheel, shaving fine particles of ice from the block clamped in place and mounding it onto spindly wooden sticks with an effortless skill born of long practice. A row of bottles framed the cart, held together with rope like a group of climbers up in the Matheran hills that Brian had visited the year before. The bottles gleamed purple, red, orange, yellow, and green, their contents a loose approximation of the flavors for which each syrup was named.

"Have you seen Hassan today?" Brian asked.

"No, son, not today. You want a gola?"

Brian shook his head. Without looking up, he navigated the chaotic universe of football, cricket, and hockey games that occupied the entirety of the playground at the same time, yet managed to maintain a semblance of order. The relentless glare of the afternoon sun assaulted his eyes, and he sighed with relief when he reached the comfort of the junior school building. At the canteen counter, he raised a hand over the tightly packed row of glass jars containing an assortment of snack foods and paid for a plate of puri bhaji. He carried the plate past the counter and across the stone steps of the assembly hall. He sat down at one of the green-topped tables that occupied a designated area during the lunch hour. The table wobbled unceremoniously on spindly, rusting legs as he set his plate on it and brushed aside the remnants of someone else's meal. A few crows eyed him from the crossbeams overhead, waiting their turn to swoop down and snatch whatever morsels they could find. Brian scooped some of the bhaji with a puri, lifted it to his mouth, and shot a quick look at a group of boys seated at the far end of the table. They ignored him, busy with their food. He wondered, yet again, whether Hassan would return soon.

Brian had first met Hassan five years earlier, days after starting school at St. Magnus. Although Brian hadn't made friends easily, he initially gravitated to a group of other Goans who introduced him to the street vendors. He learned that the vendors were a common sight along the dusty Bombay pavements, especially in the office districts and near schools. Accustomed to skirting the boundaries of legality, the vendors tolerated the occasional police raids with resignation. Their carts were designed to be folded up in a hurry if one of them sounded the alarm. The few unlucky souls who were too slow paid the usual bribe after being questioned, restoring an uneasy truce.

Hassan's repertoire, in particular, fascinated Brian, who lived in the traditional Goan culinary world of spicy pork sorpotel and vindaloos, balchao, fish curries, rice, and pickle. At first, he sampled many of Hassan's wares—tangy tamarind fruit, sweet chikki that often glued his teeth together, peppery spice balls that resembled goat droppings—but quickly settled on his favorite, aam papad. Sometimes, Brian indulged in an accompanying serving of boodi ka baal—fine threads of white cotton candy tossed with pistachio and almond slivers.

Later, Brian discovered that snacks were not the only items Hassan served on the weather-beaten tray. He also kept a small suitcase behind him, from which he withdrew a variety of trinkets upon request. The surface of the suitcase became a miniature circus stage, on which gleaming silver capsules danced in open matchboxes, tiny colored propellers launched into flight atop spiral rods, plastic dinosaurs stood frozen in time, and autographed pictures of Indian cricketers smiled out at an enthralled audience. Brian had noticed that the older boys seemed to have access to another, private collection of photographs, but he had soon lost interest after Hassan told him he was too young to appreciate them.

With a sigh, Brian turned back to his meal. Most of the conversations nearby centered around cricket. Several boys carried pocket radios with them, and the Test match commentary crackled and hissed over the sounds of clanging utensils and plates. Maybe he would find a game of cricket to join in after lunch.

Hassan ran out of Kapilgaon station, stumbling across a homeless man lying near the exit. A horde of auto rickshaws veered towards him, each driver vying for the fare by attempting to shout down the others. He got into the nearest one and gave the driver directions. The dust, noise, and smell of the train journey had left him feeling dazed, imparting a dreamlike aura to his surroundings.

The driver shook his head. "I can't take you there, sahib. Too much trouble, still, in that neighborhood."

Hassan's heart thumped with an erratic, wild rhythm. "What do you mean?"

"The riots, sahib. Many parts of the chawls burned to the ground. It is too dangerous."

Hassan swallowed, wishing he'd stopped to get some tea at the station. He didn't have the energy for an hour-long walk, especially with the afternoon heat closing around him like a vice. Already, sweat was puddling in his armpits and running down his back.

The driver coughed and spat a thin, red streak of paan juice into a deep trench in the pavement, a relic of a municipal project begun but long forgotten. "You want to go somewhere else, sahib? I will take you very fast."

Hassan nodded. He gave him the address of his uncle, who lived in a suburb of Kapilgaon, about twenty minutes from the station. Although they hadn't spoken in years, Hassan felt sure his uncle would know what to do.

The driver smiled, exposing a set of uneven, crimson teeth. "Very good, sahib. Good neighborhood. No problem at all. I will take you very fast."

Hassan barely noticed the incessant clamoring of horns as the auto rickshaw meandered through the traffic like a drunk staggering home after the country liquor dens closed. Bicycles, bullock carts, and buses that belched thick, black smoke moved in anarchic streams with the auto rickshaws and cars along the streets. Many of the shops—normally selling everything from groceries to stainless steel cookware to shoes—stood silent behind shutters and honeycomb grilles. Although Hassan could detect no other outward signs of the recent violence, the pulse of the city felt different, more muted somehow.

After a while, the bustle of the main roads gave way to lighter traffic and narrow, tree-lined lanes. A smattering of stone bungalows with carefully tended gardens broke up the orderly march of high-rise buildings. In a few houses, swings hung in front porches, largely unoccupied at this time of day. The auto rickshaw pulled over by a modest-sized house with a tan brick exterior that looked like it had just been washed.

Hassan paid the driver and walked up the worn steps. He banged the brass knocker several times.

The door opened a crack, held back by its chain, and a pair of cloudy brown eyes peered at him from behind thick glasses. "Hassan? Is it really you?"

The door closed briefly, and Hassan heard the rattle of the chain being drawn from its slot. This time, the door opened wide. "Yes, Salim uncle," he said. "It's really me."

His uncle threw his bony arms around him and ushered him in. "I'm so sorry, Hassan—I should have sent you a telegram immediately. But the way things have been here—"

Hassan's eyes took in the immaculate cut of Salim's shirt and the perfectly creased khaki trousers. Apart from cataracts in both eyes, his uncle had weathered the years well, maintaining his lean, almost athletic figure that caused Hassan's mother to fret about whether her brother was getting enough to eat every time she saw him. No doubt, Hassan thought, Salim still took his daily hour-long walk. He'd lived in the bungalow, in this sleepy neighborhood, as long as Hassan could remember. After he retired, he'd invited Hassan's parents to move in with him, but Hassan's father had refused, his pride forbidding him from accepting what he saw as an act of charity from his brother-in-law.

Salim shut the door behind them, and Hassan grabbed his arm. "My parents—what news? Have you seen them?"

Salim shook his head, leading Hassan to a wicker chair in front of a large television set. On the color screen—still a rarity in Hassan's world—the prime minister stood behind a cluster of microphones on a podium. He was describing the rapid spread of the riots and pleaded for the necessity to remain united despite religious differences. Clearly, Hassan realized, the incident was significant enough to merit national attention.

Hassan remained standing, although he felt like his knees would give way at any moment. "Tell me, Salim uncle. How bad is it?"

Once again, Salim shook his head. "I don't know, Hassan. The mobs got to them all, every single room in the chawls. They set fire to the buildings and began attacking people as they ran away from the blaze—men, women, and children. They knew no Hindus lived there. So far, nobody can tell me if your parents escaped. I've asked the police, but they have been taking their time."

Hassan collapsed in the chair, the wicker creaking in protest. "I must find them. I have to try." He buried his face in his hands for a while, fighting the sobs that welled up in his chest. On the television, a smattering of applause interrupted the prime minister's speech. "How did this happen?"

Salim shrugged. "Nobody really knows. Tensions are always high here, especially now that the local politicians are pushing their Hindu nationalist agenda. Some people say it started when a Muslim boy living on the street pissed on the wall outside the Hindu temple on Shivaji Road. A group of Hindu boys who were passing by beat him up, and it spread from there. Within hours, mobs appeared everywhere, burning houses and looting shops."

Hassan blew his nose with the cloth that he extracted from a kurta pocket. "I'll go to the chawls, start making inquiries—"

Salim placed a hand on Hassan's shoulder. "It's too dangerous. Why don't you let the police handle it for now? Stay here tonight, get some rest. Tomorrow, we'll go to the police station, okay?"

Hassan's shoulders heaved. Although he tried to tear his eyes away from the television screen, he found himself watching with a terrible fascination. The images flashed by: people running through the streets and trampling others in their efforts to escape, policemen waving their lathis and attempting to charge a crowd, roiling black smoke and angry flames consuming buildings that looked strangely familiar.

After a long silence, he raised his head and nodded.

"Hey Brian. Here's the tape."

Brian squinted at the scratched plastic case, through which he could make out the gaunt, mustached face of Freddie Mercury. He didn't know the names of the other members of Queen, but the lead singer was the subject of legend at St. Magnus. A wood desk in a third-standard classroom still bore the name Farrokh Balsara carved into its surface, though school records were unclear on exactly when he had attended St. Magnus.

"Thanks, Sohrab," he said, looking up at the boy who stood by the lunch table. "I'll get it back to you as soon as I'm done."

Sohrab nodded and sat down across from Brian. Now in his final year, Sohrab Mistry had befriended Brian from his first day of school, watching out for him at recess time and occasionally shielding him from the taunts of older students. Brian thought of Sohrab as an older brother. The bond between them grew as they found common ground in being minorities in a land where Hindu traditions were political, not just spiritual.

Sohrab stretched his long, pale arms and yawned. "No cricket today?"

Brian sighed. "Maybe later." Thanks to Sohrab's expert guidance, Brian had learned how to use a cricket bat as if it were a musical instrument, weaving compositions of delicate leg glances punctuated by powerful hook shots and cover drives.

"Sohrab, have you heard anything about Hassan?" If anyone had information, Sohrab would. "He's been missing all week. Ever since the day we heard about the riots in Kapilgaon."

Sohrab raised an eyebrow. "Doesn't he have family there? Did you ask the golawala?"

Brian squirmed on the bench, trying to ease the stiffness in his lower back. "I'm sure he went home to Kapilgaon, but the golawala hasn't heard anything."

That night, Hassan tossed and turned even though the blanket of white noise from the window air-conditioner muffled the unfamiliar sounds of suburbia. The occasional barking of stray dogs filtered through, along with the now infrequent horns of nighttime traffic. After a while, he swung his legs over the side of the bed and peered at the clock on his nightstand. It was a few minutes past midnight. He stood up and stretched, trying to expel the ordeal of the day's journey in one long breath. He slipped his feet into the leather sandals waiting by the bedside.

Two auto rickshaws were parked at the street corner, but the first driver was curled up in his seat, snoring. The second, after a prolonged session of haggling, finally agreed to take Hassan to a location within two kilometers of the chawls. Hassan slumped back in his seat as the driver executed a U-turn and the three-wheeled vehicle wobbled, hesitated, and then shot forward. He didn't really know what he would do once he made it to the chawls—or what was left of them. He just knew he had to get there.

The auto rickshaw set Hassan down at Palsule Chowk, halfway between the railroad station and the older part of the city where the chawls proliferated in untidy heaps along narrow streets. He paid the driver and set off at a brisk pace, encountering nothing of note other than a few stray dogs. They followed him for a while but turned and ran when they realized he had no food to offer. Behind him, the moon hung low in the sky, painting the landscape ahead in shades of silver and gray. He walked on, taking slow, ragged breaths.

The lane leading into the chawls lay somber and still, devoid of the thin strands of early morning energy that normally wound along it. The first two buildings stood like battered, smoking sentries on either side of the lane as Hassan approached.

Hassan remembered how the chawls had buzzed with activity, even at two in the morning when his father came home from his shift at the textile mills. His mother would be asleep on the cot his parents shared in the one-room dwelling. She always took the spot along the wall. Hassan had a smaller cot placed against the opposite wall, leaving a narrow walkway between them. Some nights when he couldn't sleep, he heard his father moving about in the kitchen, behind the thin curtain that separated it from the rest of the living space. Then his father crept into bed, trying not to wake them. After he heard his parents snoring, Hassan got up and walked through the door into the common balcony that stretched across all the rooms on the floor. Although he knew it would be difficult to get up in time for school the next day, he stayed on the balcony for a while, the throbbing energy of the chawls filling his veins as he watched traffic ebb and flow. Shutters veiled the shops on the ground floor across the lane, and only a few lights flickered here and there, probably other mill workers like his father. At length, he lay down on the threadbare blanket that covered the floor of the balcony and drifted off, comforted by the familiar noises of the city slowly emerging from its slumber. He awoke to find his mother shaking him by the shoulder. Hazy sunlight diffused through the smoke that rose from fires scattered throughout the chawls. The acrid smell of burning garbage would mingle with the more savory aroma of coal-fired stoves cooking the first meal of the day.

Now a different, harsher smoke permeated everything. It tore at the back of his throat and cried out to him with the voices of the victims it had claimed. The balconies were gone, consumed by the fire, except for a few charred columns that hung at odd angles like broken bones. Fragments of shattered glass clung to some of the narrow windows. The concrete and iron framework of the chawls remained, like the skeleton of a hollowed-out corpse, still rising four stories into the sky. The main staircase at the center of each chawl gaped at him, issuing a silent invitation.

Hassan walked to the familiar building, the third on the right. He pictured it as he'd seen it last: laundry drying over the balcony rails, flower garlands hanging above the brightly colored doors from which paint peeled in thick, heavy flakes, and neighbors gathering in balconies to exchange gossip and food.

His heart beat faster as he approached the entrance. He paused at the foot of the stairs. The open courtyard at the core of the chawl used to be the center of social activity. It hosted innumerable games of cricket and football, festival celebrations, and impromptu gatherings to rejoice in births and weddings or to mourn a death. The bonds that developed in the community knit the residents together into a resilient fabric. As a boy, he'd always thought it would be tough enough to withstand anything. Tears burned like acid as they streaked down his soot-covered cheeks. He took a gulp of air and coughed, wiping his eyes with the sleeve of his kurta. As he continued up the stairs, which had survived the flames except for the cheap wood railings, he hesitated. He hadn't really expected to find anyone in the wreckage—Salim had told him that the police had cleared away the bodies day before. Yet some force that he didn't quite understand propelled him onto the landing at the second floor and down the narrow hallway toward the common latrines.

Instead of the door, a heap of debris and ash greeted him. He stepped over the threshold and shivered as he surveyed the room. Whatever personal effects had survived the fire must have fallen prey to looters, as nothing but blackened walls and the twisted steel frames of two cots remained. The narrow shelf above the kitchen stove, where his parents stored their meager belongings, was bare except for a jumble of timbers from the ceiling that had partially caved in.

For the first time, Hassan realized the danger posed by the decrepit building. The chawls were almost a century old, and patchy maintenance had not reinforced the soundness of the structure. What was left after the fire could collapse at any moment. With one last searching look at the ghost of a place he had known the better part of his life, Hassan turned away.

As he passed the courtyard, he noticed the glint of moonlight on metal in a corner. He walked through piles of rubble and broken glass. A few cooking utensils lay scattered in front of a mound of bricks. An arm, blackened and twisted, stuck out from under the pile. Hassan squatted low, unable to let his knees touch the ground. With shaking hands, he began to remove bricks from the top of the heap. As he leaned forward, a hand fell on his shoulder. He spun around, his heart pounding.

Three men faced him. The closest one grabbed him, pulling him to his feet. Hassan couldn't see the faces of the others, but he caught the unmistakable silhouette of a knife blade. Trembling, he raised his head to peer at the man who still held his shoulder in a grip of steel. The man's eyes, narrow slits that glistened with cold rage, seemed to search Hassan's soul.

"What are you doing here?" His voice sent a chill up Hassan's spine. "There is nothing left to loot. We cleaned the place out yesterday." He towered above Hassan by almost half a meter. In the half-shadows of the moonlight, Hassan noticed the bulge of muscles beneath a tattered undershirt. He exuded a raw, commanding energy, like a panther ready to pounce. Clearly, this man was in charge of the group. He came closer, and his eyebrows knit together. "Where do you live?"

Behind the leader, Hassan heard the others whispering the word he dreaded: mussalmaan. They came forward, peering at him with bloodshot eyes. "Mussalmaan," they said again.

Hassan threw up his hands, twisting his body to break free, but the leader only tightened his hold on Hassan's shoulder. "Friends, this is a misunderstanding. I am Hindu, like you. I am a poor man who lives nearby, and I came here to see if I could find something to sell. It will help me feed my family.

I will go now, as there is nothing here for me." He tried to take a step back.

The leader drew him forward until their noses almost touched. "You are lying, you swine."

"Pull down his pants," shouted one of the other men. "We'll settle this soon enough."

The leader spun Hassan around, then pinned his hands behind his back as the other two advanced. The one with the knife held it to Hassan's throat. He felt the tip of the blade, cold as ice against his skin. The other man ripped his pants down with a swift movement, and they pooled around his ankles. He stared straight ahead, trying not to show the fear that paralyzed him.

"Mussalmaan!" they shouted. "Kill him, quick!" The knife flashed high in the air, and a red-hot pain tore through Hassan's shoulder like a fiery arrow. Blood gushed out, soaking the front of his kurta. In the distance, he thought he heard muffled shouts. His legs collapsed under him, and he slid to the ground. Then someone kicked him in the head. For a moment, it seemed like the world around him exploded with flashes of brightly colored light. He groaned as the fire in his shoulder began to spread, consuming his body. Gradually, the light faded and merciful darkness claimed him.

When he woke, a different light—cold, white, and diffuse—made his eyes water. This time, however, he could make out blurred shapes around him. His uncle's face floated above him, distorted and shimmering, like a reflection in a puddle. He heard muted beeps and a low, mechanical humming. The faint sting of antiseptic in the air that he sucked into his lungs told him he was in a hospital bed.

Slowly, his uncle's face came into focus. "I'm glad you're awake, Hassan." He mopped his forehead with a pale blue handkerchief. "You were very lucky that a few policemen were still patrolling the chawls. If they hadn't shown up at the right time, I wouldn't be talking to you now. What were you doing there, anyway?"

Hassan raised his right hand, noting with a muddled detachment the tubes and wires that sprouted from his arm. With a deep sigh, he let it fall back onto the bed by his side. He tried to move his left arm and sit up, but a sharp, stabbing pain in his chest made him abandon the effort. A wave of nausea washed over him as he recalled the sneering faces and the taunts of the men. "I don't know," he whispered. "I just had to see for myself."

Brian walked through the gates with his head bowed. He didn't expect this day to be any different from the past three weeks. Then, as he got closer, he glimpsed sunlight reflecting off an aluminum tray. He broke into a run, elbowing his way through the crowd.

"Hassan! I'm so glad you're back. What happened to you? Did you go home to Kapilgaon?"

He saw a brief glimpse of the familiar, crooked smile, but then it seemed as if a cloud cast a dark shadow over Hassan's face. He noticed Hassan's left arm was in a sling.

"I did go home, son. It was a family emergency." Hassan peeled a sheet of plastic away from the tray, exposing a half-wheel of cashew chikki. "I'm back now. I'm sorry, but I don't have any aam papad today."

A Different Music

I T'S A SILLY RITUAL, I know. I'm almost embarrassed to be
writing about it. An hour before the first members of the
orchestra arrive, when the concert hall is quiet except for
the cleaning crew, I sit down at the piano. I reflect on what the
day will bring, and I play *Chopsticks*. Variations on *Chopsticks*.
Like most rituals, this one comforts me, grounds me in the
present, and helps me focus. Today, especially, I need to focus.
My father called this morning with the news that Mr. Watson
had died.

At the age of seventy-two, he lost his final battle. Cancer
ravaged his body for several years but could never claim his
mind. Mr. Watson—I still want to call him "Sir," even though
it's been many years since I wore the school uniform—was
not a musician. However, he influenced me more than any
musician has ever done. He gave me a deep, abiding love for
the English language that persists to this day. And, in his years
as principal of St. Magnus, he guided a generation of boys
through challenges, triumphs, and torments as they crossed
the threshold into young adulthood.

Mr. Watson taught me to follow my passion, even though I think he secretly hoped I'd become an English teacher like him. Before I left Bombay for the precollege program at Juilliard, we met at a small Irani restaurant not too far from the school. As we sat there, drinking hot, milky tea from glasses while we waited for lunch, he told me I should never give up on my dreams. Then he announced he was going to retire from St. Magnus, at the age of sixty.

"Why now?" I asked. "You could keep going for a few more years."

"It's time," he said, his voice tinged with regret, "to walk away."

"But sir...you're just going to let them win?"

He blew on his tea, sending tendrils of steam in my direction like outstretched fingers. "Perhaps they win, but it doesn't mean I lose."

"What will you do now? Surely you can find another position—"

"Actually, I have a better plan." I could sense a lightness in his voice, now that he'd broken the news. "I've decided to become an English tutor. A few parents at St. Magnus have already asked me to enroll their sons, and I have no doubt I will keep busy for quite some time."

Cancer was by no means the least of the trials Mr. Watson faced. The events leading up to his retirement stretched back for years, but I think the turning point came about in a single day.

Boys were milling around everywhere that day, as I ran past the school clerk's desk on my way to Mr. Watson's office. He burst through the crowd, shouting, "Get some buckets—the bastards have set my office on fire!" A few of us ran to the janitor's room where we found a bag of sand that we passed to Mr. Watson. I recruited a group of other tenth-standard students who collected tin pails that we took to the bathroom down the hall. We filled them with water and formed a makeshift bucket brigade, with Mr. Watson at the tail end.

We managed to put the fire out in just a few minutes. Apparently, it had started in his wastebasket. I wondered whether he had accidentally left a cigarette on his desk and it had fallen off the edge, but it wasn't like him to do so. Careful, tidy almost to the point of obsessive fastidiousness, he would never have put a cigarette in anything except his ashtray.

As I stood there, surrounded by smoky, water-soaked chaos, he caught my eye. "Come here, Mistry," he said. He swept his arm in a wide arc, encompassing the skeleton of the desk, the piles of sand, and puddles of water covering most of the floor. "You see what they've done now. They're trying to force me out." Behind the trademark horn-rimmed glasses, his eyes were bloodshot and held a weariness I wasn't accustomed to seeing.

At the time, I wondered why he hadn't given up earlier. After all, a man with his credentials could walk into a similar job anywhere in Bombay. Later, I realized it was more than just a job to him. In spite of constant opposition, he struggled to hang on to what he loved most.

Mr. Watson was the only non-Jesuit to hold the position of principal in the history of St. Magnus. For almost twelve years, he'd been an English teacher, and for five of those years, an assistant principal. The Jesuits guarded their realm with a ferocious, unwavering zeal. It was unthinkable that someone outside their order, much less a layperson, would ever ascend to the throne at St. Magnus. Yet the impossible happened: the previous principal appointed Mr. Watson his successor when he retired. He did this partly in a fit of spite at his comrades, with whom he rarely agreed, and partly because he knew Mr. Watson would make a better principal than any of the others who aspired to that highest of high posts at the time.

Father Bosco, the heir apparent, was a history teacher who had established seniority. A Jesuit who emigrated from Spain, he possessed a large, bulbous head that seemed to be in constant danger of toppling from his spindly body. A sadistic streak ran through him, and he took great pleasure in ruling with an iron fist and imparting his particular brand of physical discipline. When he succeeded Mr. Watson as assistant principal, canings increased substantially. Although Mr. Watson tried to fire Father Bosco on more than one occasion, the Jesuits—true to a man—rallied behind him and wielded sufficient power with the bishop that he remained at his post.

The one decision Father Bosco could not reverse, of course, was the appointment of Mr. Watson as principal. Even though it was highly irregular, the outgoing principal's nomination was final and binding. Not that it stopped Father Bosco from challenging it, but on this front the bishop remained unmoved.

So the battle raged. The Jesuits never lost an opportunity, great or small, to malign Mr. Watson's reputation. Such was the quality of his character, however, that he bore each insult with a grace that shamed his opponents. The band of priests didn't seem to realize that each incident only endeared Mr. Watson further to his students and to the laypeople who formed the majority of the school's teachers and staff.

That strength of character permeated everything Mr. Watson did. In my last year at St. Magnus, I qualified for the final eleven of the annual Staff vs. Students cricket match. The event took place on the larger of the two school grounds, and students and teachers alike gathered along the perimeter for the spectacle. Others crowded around their classroom windows. The grounds were smaller than a regulation stadium, and a six usually meant losing the ball on the busy road that bounded the north side of the school, or on the railway tracks to the west. The pitch itself—a coir mat stretched tight over the bumpy, stone-riddled soil—would have been unplayable in any real match. Yet these irregularities did little to quench the tremendous enthusiasm that the players exhibited, and the audience cheered as lustily as if they were watching an India-Pakistan World Cup final.

We were batting second in the twenty-over game, chasing an impressive total of 167 for 7 by the staff. We'd just lost our third wicket, and I had been promoted in the batting order by our captain in an attempt to accelerate the run rate. My classmate, Sanjay, was at bat; I stood, tense and poised for a quick single, at the non-striker's end. Mr. Watson had the ball and began his run up. As he neared the stumps, I moved forward without a second thought, and my bat left the safety of the crease. I heard the familiar voice shout, "Get back at once, Mistry!" I spun around to see Mr. Watson paused in mid-stride, and I scrambled back to my former position. With one flick of his wrist, he could have broken the wicket, and I would have been run out. Instead, he gave me a look that made me feel like a first-standard student again and began walking back to start his run-up afresh.

It didn't matter in the grand scheme of things, as we ended up losing the match by ten runs anyway. After it was over and the trophy presented, I sought out Mr. Watson. "Why didn't you run me out when you had the chance, sir? It would have been perfectly legal, according to the rules."

He looked at me with a smile that I still remember and ran a finger along his impeccably trimmed mustache. "Cricket is about a lot more than playing by the rules, Mistry. It's a gentleman's game. Don't you ever forget that."

During middle school, our relationship grew beyond the confines of the school grounds, largely thanks to my father. He took a tremendous liking to Mr. Watson and frequently issued him invitations to dinner. It may seem strange for a schoolboy to look forward to interacting on a social level with his principal, but I enjoyed those occasions. We rarely sat down to meals as a family, since my father worked long hours at the shoe manufacturing company he owned. He generally came home after the servants had cleared the table. Somehow, he always managed to make time for dinner when he knew Mr. Watson would be joining us.

While my mother orchestrated the activity in the kitchen, they'd sit on the sofa, my father with his Scotch, Mr. Watson with a gin and tonic. Sometimes, they argued the relative merits of obscure Victorian novelists or discussed the quirks of fate that drove Shakespeare to be as prolific as he was. Mostly, they sat with their eyes closed in companionable silence, sipping their drinks and absorbing a Beethoven symphony or a Mozart concerto with every fiber of their being.

I found it odd, even a little annoying, that Mr. Watson never asked me to play the piano, as most of our other dinner guests did. Since the age of eight, I'd become accustomed to performing on demand for my mother, my aunts and uncles, and miscellaneous other wanderers through the Mistry household. Perhaps he didn't want to embarrass me. For some time, I feared I simply wouldn't live up to his standards, and maybe it was better that I never had to prove myself to him. Yet, when I received my acceptance letter from Juilliard and the word spread within hours through my mother's social connections, Mr. Watson was the first to call and congratulate me.

My mother sometimes hired an additional cook to help out with the lavish array of dishes. In addition to the Parsi staples—dhansakh, khichri, sali murghi—she often included her variations on Mughlai cuisine. On a few occasions, we were joined by my aunt Zulma, who flirted outrageously with Mr. Watson but never seemed to evoke the slightest bit of interest from him. He'd made it clear he was a confirmed bachelor and intended to stay that way. To be honest, I think she scared him, just a little. She had that effect on most men.

One night, after the servants had cleared the dishes and my father had brought out a fine selection of after-dinner liqueurs, Mr. Watson told us about the latest salvo fired by the priests at St. Magnus. Earlier in the week, he'd been busy with teachers' meetings and stayed late to finish meticulous preparations for his English class the following day. When he left his office and walked along the stone path to where he'd parked his scooter, he found it lying on its side with the tires slashed. He trudged back to his office and called his sister, who drove all the way from Bandra to pick him up. He hated taxis and buses.

He had contemplated the only practical alternative—walking fifteen or twenty minutes to the Dockyard train station—but his distaste for the overcrowded, smelly trains and their equally smelly occupants proved too much of an obstacle. The next day, a mechanic came to the school to replace the tires. Fortunately, the scooter sustained no other damage.

"This is ridiculous," my father said. "Look, Charles, I know some good lawyers. Pretty much have to, in my line of work, even though I despise their shriveled, twisted souls. Why don't you hire one and sue these buggers?"

Mr. Watson regarded him with a quiet, pensive stare, swirling the green liqueur in his glass. At length, he spoke. "I don't know if it would help."

My father shook his head. "I know you don't want to make trouble, but how can you let them get away with this shit?"

Mr. Watson sighed, leaned back, and drained his glass. He waved away my father's offer of a refill, then looked at me with an expression I found hard to read. "As long as I can continue teaching these boys, give them an appreciation for the English language, it doesn't matter what the Jesuits do to me."

He wasn't a pacifist, although it may sound like it—in fact, he had an uncommon dislike for Gandhian principles. I'd seen him intervene in fights often enough, typically to protect a younger student from bullies. And I heard he'd been quite adept at boxing in his own school days at St. Magnus. I never understood the sport's appeal, but I liked to picture Mr. Watson in the ring, with a referee holding up his gloved hand. The image offered a pleasant incongruence with my early impressions of him.

*

I first met Mr. Watson at our class Christmas party. This tradition distinguished the first standard from the rest of the school: although we continued to have Christmas parties through the next few standards, the celebrations were different. It didn't matter if you weren't a Christian—you participated in the whole affair anyway. It began with the Christmas story, read by the teacher with a little help from the advanced readers in the class. Next, we made decorations—red and green paper chains, streamers that twirled across the room, painted styrofoam baubles that were destined to adorn an artificial tree. Most importantly, each one of us made his own paper hat. The teacher asked us to prepare extras, but we weren't told why.

After we ravaged a tray of suitably festive snacks like locusts stripping a farm field, our teacher announced that the principal, Father Dias, was going to visit and we had better behave, or else. A buzz of anticipation filled the classroom—we'd been hoping for Santa Claus, but the principal would have to do. A few minutes later, instead of the principal, Mr. Watson stepped into the room. He apologized for Father Dias' inability to keep the appointment, acknowledging that the assistant principal was a poor substitute. A couple of our other teachers accompanied him: Mr. Rego, the math teacher, and Mrs. Sheth, the Hindi teacher who doubled as an art instructor. The classroom conversation died down right away, which seemed to surprise Mr. Watson. He waved a hand and told us to carry on, but we still spoke in whispers.

Mr. Watson donned one of the paper hats as if such embellishments were a regular part of his wardrobe. He spent a few minutes walking around the classroom, asking questions here, praising artistic efforts there, and soon we were very much at ease in his presence. Then we took our places in front of the blackboard, lining up in rows for the class picture. Mr. Watson stood at the rear with the other teachers, resplendent in his jacket, tie, and paper hat. After the photograph, he thanked us for the invitation and moved on to the next classroom, presumably to go through the same ritual.

Even though I only exchanged a few words with Mr. Watson that day, his quiet dignity struck a chord. To be sure, he commanded respect by virtue of his position, but he wore the mantle of responsibility lightly. Subsequent encounters—even an occasion when I was sent to his office for disciplinary measures beyond those which my teacher could exert—only reinforced my first impressions. Most of the students I knew, in all class levels, held Mr. Watson in high regard not because of his rank, but because to do so otherwise would diminish us, not him.

Years later, in the fifth standard, I experienced the unexpected pleasure of Mr. Watson teaching my English class, just for a day. Our regular English teacher, we learned, had succumbed to a nasty bout of the flu and decided to recuperate at home. Mr. Watson asked us to open our English literature textbook to the previous lesson, an excerpt from *Around the World in Eighty Days*. Our teacher had assigned some homework questions, largely delving into the motivations of Phineas Fogg, so Mr. Watson began by asking a few of us to read our responses. Then he cleared his throat, closed the book, and tossed it onto the teacher's desk.

"Pretty dry stuff, eh?" His eyes swept the classroom as he leaned back in his chair. He stood up and walked to the blackboard. "What do you boys like to read?"

For a while, we sat there in stunned silence, not knowing what the appropriate responses should be. He prompted us again, and after giving it some thought, we began to reply with increasing enthusiasm. Comic books, especially *Asterix* and *TinTin*. *The Hardy Boys*. *The Lone Pine* series by Malcolm Saville. *The Three Investigators* series.

Mr. Watson wrote all these on the blackboard, as each hand was raised and the answer volunteered, in beautifully scripted, precise letters. In a few minutes, he filled almost the entire board. He stood to the side, looking over all the entries, seemingly lost in thought. Then he took a seat at the desk and faced the class.

"Quite a variety we have here," he said, his glasses glinting in the overhead fluorescent light. "Have any of you boys heard of a gentleman named William Shakespeare?"

A few hands went up, mine included.

"How about Charles Dickens?" Two or three more hands reached for the ceiling.

"Shaw? Hemingway? Hardy?" In rapid-fire succession, we responded as best as we could.

"Now tell me, have any of you actually read anything by Shakespeare?"

This time, the class sat still. Not a single hand moved.

"Of course you haven't," he said, removing his glasses and polishing them with a white handkerchief that he extracted from his shirt pocket. "You're too young! Someday, God willing, you will take my tenth-standard class and have the pleasure of studying Shakespeare." He waved a chalk-dusted hand at the blackboard and walked back to his seat. "Can you tell me one thing Shakespeare, Dickens, and Hardy have in common that these others don't?"

We pondered the question for a while, and I stole a quick glance at my classmates. Nobody seemed ready with an answer, so I raised a shaky hand. "Please, sir, they're all...dead?"

He looked at me for a moment, a frown building on his forehead. My ears began to burn as I lowered my hand. Then his lips quivered, and he roared with laughter, rocking back and forth in his chair. "Why, so they are," he said. He came over to my desk and patted me on the shoulder. "They are indeed. Capital observation, eh?"

As he returned to the blackboard, I heard him muttering to himself, "They're all dead. Excellent, eh? They're all dead."

In the tenth standard, I did take the promised English class. Although Mr. Watson was principal by then, he hadn't relinquished all his teaching duties. He shared the responsibility for teaching the three tenth-standard divisions with Mrs. Sengupta, a large woman with a strong Bengali accent whose waist-length hair glistened with coconut oil. Accustomed to the role of matriarch in her family of ten, she saw the classroom as her dominion to be ruled with an imperial disdain. Fortunately, I happened to be in the division that belonged to Mr. Watson.

His approach to teaching Shakespeare surprised me. It certainly didn't follow the guide books, and a handful of the students complained he wasn't preparing them for the final exams. These constituted a statewide trial by fire that all of us would undergo at the end of the school year and whose grades would largely determine our admission to junior college. But rather than have us parrot answers to simplistic questions, as all the exam prep guides dictated, Mr. Watson delved into history and setting. He displayed a comfortable intimacy with the characters in Julius Caesar, making the play come alive. When he read an excerpt, I could almost picture the overhead lights dimming and the floodlights fixing him in their glare. The class sat in hushed silence, and even the air itself seemed still, paying homage to the masterful performance taking place.

And so was born my love of Shakespeare. Since then, I've had the opportunity to see some of the great actors on stage as I've traveled the world. Each experience takes me back to that sweltering classroom in the tenth standard—Mr. Watson had a peculiar aversion to the ceiling fans that provided feeble relief from the oppressive Bombay heat. His pure, unadulterated joy of the English language infected many of us, a disease no inoculation could prevent.

In my final term at St. Magnus, the movement to oust Mr. Watson reached its peak, with the arson attempt being the culmination of Father Bosco's diabolical yet clumsy schemes. The next offensive proved less clumsy.

Father Bosco managed the teaching schedule for the upper school each term. He typically posted it the week before finals on the bulletin boards outside the teachers' common room.

We heard the news during geography class. Mrs. Ferraro, a silver-haired, sari-clad Goan woman with an acid tongue was holding forth on the climate of the African savannah when the school clerk beckoned to her from the doorway. She flung the stick of chalk she was holding at the narrow shelf below the blackboard, from where it rolled onto the floor and broke into three pieces. As she stormed out of the room, I felt a twinge of sympathy for Stanley, the hapless clerk. We strained our ears to catch the conversation, but we didn't have long to wait.

A few minutes later Mrs. Ferraro returned, all traces of her former irritation erased. In its stead, a steely light shone in her eyes. She stood facing us, hands on hips, her sari billowing in the wind that rushed through the open window on the far side of the classroom. "Boys, we will have to finish our discussion next time. The Tyrant has decreed that Mr. Watson shall no longer teach his tenth-standard English class. In fact, he has removed Mr. Watson's name from all his English class schedules—eighth, ninth, and tenth standards."

A murmur rose from the students and grew into a roar as the full import of her announcement sank in. Mrs. Ferraro raised a hand, and the class fell silent. "You fellows wait here for a minute. I told Stanley to spread the word to the other tenth-standard students. I'm going to run down to the eighth and ninth standards, and I'll be back shortly. We won't let the Tyrant get away with this, I assure you."

When she returned, most of us were on our feet. We poured out into the hallway with Mrs. Ferraro in the lead. The other tenth-standard divisions joined us, and soon we were marching downstairs to Father Bosco's office. Along the way, a stream of eighth- and ninth-standard students joined the rushing torrent that spilled out across the worn gray and black stone staircase. Carried along with the current, I found myself near the front lines, where several teachers sustained a noble but ineffectual effort to maintain discipline. Once again, Mrs.

Ferraro commanded silence with a raised hand and knocked on the office door. It opened to admit her while we waited outside, passing information in whispers down the line.

After an eternity, the door creaked open, and Father Bosco emerged with Mrs. Ferraro close behind. He took one look at the packed hallway, rushed back into his office, and slammed the door. The next day, we saw that a revised schedule had been posted on the bulletin board, with Mr. Watson's name taking its rightful place.

Mr. Watson endured these trials with a stoic courage that surprised many students. At first, I wondered if it was a product of his Anglo-Indian heritage. Through the years, however, I realized he also derived strength from deep religious convictions.

Although a devout Catholic, Mr. Watson never imposed his beliefs on us, even in an environment where evangelism flourished. Once a week, Catholic students took compulsory religious education classes run by the Jesuits, while the rest of us were instructed in what was called "moral science"—a dreadful mishmash of formless ideas that promised to improve our relationships "with God, our fellowmen, and ourselves," as the syllabus said. In the ninth standard, though, Mr. Watson taught the class and turned it into an introduction to philosophy. We discussed ethics, free will and determinism, and the origins of religion. More than just a lecture, the class encouraged discussion and debate in a way that no others did—Mr. Watson demanded that we question everything. I looked forward to that class every week, as did a few other boys who, in retrospect, may have been somewhat advanced for their age.

Perhaps those classes inspired my eventual rise to leadership of the House debate team. Four Houses, each branded with a different color, divided the school for all competitive events. Mine—the Green House—advanced to the debate finals. Fresh off our semifinal victory, we gathered in Mr. Watson's office to set the stage for the showdown against our archrivals, the Red House. Since we won our previous matchup by a wider point margin than the Red House team, we earned the right to draw the topic from a hat.

We found Mr. Watson pacing in his office, muttering to himself, a sure sign that he'd had a run-in with Fr. Bosco. "He wanted to see the topic list," he said, his eyes glittering. "He wanted to censor topics he found inappropriate or offensive. I refused."

We looked at the hat that sat on his desk. It really was a hat—a stiff, black top hat with a broad silk band. "What is the theme this year, sir?" I asked. He always had a theme.

"I decided to pick famous headlines from newspapers and magazines from the sixties. Cover stories, articles that are still remembered today, that sort of thing. Not just our Indian press, you understand. I think we have a good mix of international magazines as well."

He nodded at me, and I reached into the hat, pulling out a neatly folded slip of paper about as long as my middle finger. I unfolded it and read it aloud. " 'Is God dead?' "

His eyes lost some of their sharpness, and a mischievous smile curled a corner of his mouth. "*Time* magazine, I believe, some time in 1966. Oh, I think the priests would certainly like to censor that one."

The news spread faster than a kerosene spill on a rain-slicked road. Students chuckled or groaned, parents applauded or protested, and through it all, Mr. Watson held firm. The debate would proceed with the chosen topic.

That afternoon, the auditorium was packed with students and parents alike. We even hosted a few students from neighboring schools who had been bussed in for the event.

All these factors combined to give me an almost unshakeable case of the nerves as I waited for the debate to begin, legs trembling, in a folding chair on the stage. I felt like I was going to throw up, and by the looks of it, my two teammates weren't doing much better. I steadied my breathing, forcing myself to concentrate on the intricate carvings on the wall separating the balcony from the rest of the auditorium. I tried to avoid looking at the judges who sat in the special row of cushioned seats immediately below the balcony's overhang. Gradually, the nausea began to dissipate as Mr. Watson stepped up to the microphone. He introduced the teams and called on me to open the debate as the leader of the proposition. I licked my lips, almost blinded by the footlights shining directly in my eyes. The buzzer sounded, and I launched into my opening argument.

I honestly don't remember much, if anything, of that argument today. All I know is that, from the moment I started speaking, my nerves settled and before long I was in my stride, beginning to enjoy myself immensely. The debate raged back and forth from that point. Our opponents were sharper than a Gurkha's kukri, and we couldn't afford the slightest misstep. In the end, we triumphed by a narrow margin of five points.

After the awards ceremony, I asked Mr. Watson which side he would have chosen. He didn't answer, staring at something behind me. I turned around to see Father Bosco near the judges' seats, arms crossed, with a look on his face that could have set the entire room ablaze.

A brief chuckle escaped Mr. Watson's lips. "Do you really have to ask, Sohrab?" It was one of the few times I'd heard him use my first name.

He laid a hand on my shoulder as we walked toward the exit. "Always pick the side that is the exact opposite of what you believe in your heart. It's the only way to understand what makes people like him"—he nodded at the still-fuming priest—"close their minds. And, by attempting to understand them, maybe you will find something else they lack. Forgiveness."

The remaining members of the orchestra take their places now, and the discordant wail of instruments being tuned fills the concert hall. I rest my hands lightly on the keys for a moment. Fragments of a melody drift through my head: the theme from the third movement of Beethoven's Symphony No. 9. I see a familiar face, eyes closed behind horn-rimmed glasses, enraptured by the beauty of the music. A tear runs down his cheek as he lifts a glass to his lips.

Minutes melt away in an instant, and soon it is time. The faint buzz from the audience fades. I rise to my feet as the conductor takes his post.

After the last notes drift away like specks of dust caught in a beam of sunlight, I rise again from the piano bench.

The conductor extends his hand, and I take a bow. As the applause swells to a crescendo, I bow again. This time, my audience is a million miles away.

Independence Day

ANNIE ROSE EARLY, without the aid of the alarm clock that normally sat on her nightstand. She'd packed the clock with the rest of her possessions and the movers had carried them away the day before. Only a small beige suitcase, ripped and patched in a few spots, waited by her bedside for those last-minute items she would need.

She took great care, while she made a last trip around the flat, to check each piece of furniture for items hidden in dark crevices. As she headed back to her bedroom, the doorbell rang.

Selwyn strode into the flat and gave Annie a hug. She clung to him, not wanting to let go, breathing in the familiar scent of Old Spice. As always, it reminded her of Clive.

At last, he held her at arm's length as he surveyed the living room. "You ready, ma?"

Annie tried to keep her voice steady. "Just give me a minute."

Selwyn followed her into the bedroom. "Hard to believe I lived here for over twenty years." After Annie transferred the solitary pile of clothing and toiletries from the nightstand to the suitcase, she zipped it shut and stood up, leaning on Selwyn's shoulder.

"That should be it."

Selwyn nodded. "It's a good thing the Menezes family decided to buy the furniture. Saved us a lot of trouble."

They passed the antique showcase in the living room—a gift from Annie's mother—and Selwyn commented on the barren glass shelves that shone from their recent scrubbing with Brasso. A flood of memories rushed through Annie's mind as the dam broke. She gasped for breath in between great, heaving sobs, tears tracing meandering paths down her sunken cheeks.

Once again, Selwyn took her in his arms. "It's okay, ma," he whispered. "Think of how much Ritu and the kids are looking forward to seeing you. You won't be alone anymore."

Annie managed a few sniffles in response, burying her face further in Selwyn's chest. Three years should be long enough. Yet the flat was such an integral part of her life with Clive that she couldn't quite let it go. She forced herself to think about her grandchildren, especially baby Dominic and his gaping, toothless smile. He would be the center of her universe from now on. Clive would understand.

She blew her nose with a lace-edged handkerchief. She always kept one in the pocket of her skirt. She had stitched them herself with the sewing machine that Clive…but better not to think of that now. "I'm ready. Let's go."

As they emerged from the building, Selwyn pointed out the gleaming white Ambassador waiting at the curb. Annie frowned. "I thought we were going to take the train."

"Don't worry, ma. They don't need any of the company cars today. Besides, you know how much Vijay enjoys driving. When he heard I was coming into Bombay today, he insisted."

Annie smiled at Vijay, who greeted her with folded hands and a sideways head shake. Despite the holiday, he still wore his spotless, starched white uniform. He placed Annie's suitcase into the trunk and opened the rear door for her with a magnificent bow. Annie saw Selwyn give the building a lingering look before he slid into the plush leather seat beside her. He took her hand, drawing a watery smile from her. He and Vijay discussed the best routes to avoid the parades that would be held all day.

The radio came to life as Vijay started the car. The prime minister's voice crackled and sputtered as he delivered his address to the nation from the historic Red Fort in Agra. Every year, on the fifteenth of August, Annie and Clive had gathered around their transistor radio to hear the speech. For Clive, it had been a ritual that set the tone for the day. Although Annie had paid scant attention and often dozed off for a few minutes without Clive noticing, she had derived a simple pleasure from the significance it held for him.

The Ambassador crawled through the throngs of people spilling over from the pavement on Clare Road, emerging at last into the even greater chaos of the intersection with Sankli Street and JJ Road. Vijay honked at a handcart driver who refused to yield, shaking his fist at them and cursing in Marathi. Paying no attention to the cacophony of horns, Vijay eased the car up the sloping ramp onto the Byculla flyover. A blanket of silence shrouded the market that drew visitors from all over the city, now closed for the holiday. The raw, swamp-like odor of overripe vegetables swirled around the Ambassador, and Annie glanced out the window with a twinge of regret, wrinkling her nose. It was another reminder of the world she was leaving behind.

Annie sighed as she checked the bag of tomatoes, holding it aloft like a Mughal warrior displaying the severed head of a vanquished enemy. "You're trying to throw in some of those rotten ones," she said, wagging a finger at the old man who stood behind the rickety wooden counter, eyes downcast. "What do you think I am? Yes, I'm old, but I'm not a fool."

With muttered apologies, the vendor set the bag aside and began piling a fresh batch of tomatoes on the battered, rust-flaked iron scale. Annie watched, frowning with concentration as he added each one, firing staccato objections as she discovered a tomato that failed her exacting standards. Finally, with just over two kilos completed to her satisfaction, she nodded and handed over a stash of worn rupee notes. She moved down the row of stalls and carts, jostling other customers and trying to avoid unwitting jabs from bony elbows.

She stopped at a cart piled with citrus fruit. "Arrey memsahib," the man said, a huge smile bisecting his gaunt face. "I am so happy to see you. I did not think you would come so late in the morning."

"It's probably my last chance, Suresh," Annie replied, adjusting the straps of her shopping bag.

His smile vanished. "What's wrong, memsahib? Why do you say that?"

Annie picked through a pile of sweet limes before answering. "I'm moving next week. I'll be living with my son and his family in Thana. They had a baby after a long time—their third child—and they were going to hire an ayah to take care of him during the day." She nodded at the sweet limes. "I'll take two kilos of mosambi."

Suresh sorted through the bright yellow fruit under Annie's watchful eyes and placed a handful on the scales. "You will be happy there, no? With your grandchildren?"

Annie shielded her eyes from the sun's glare with one hand. "I've lived in Byculla all my life. Even after my husband died, I didn't think of moving. Everything I need is here. But the children need me, too. And how long can I live in that big, empty flat?"

Suresh lifted the scales and added a few more mosambis to the pan so that it tipped below the counterweights. "I will miss you, memsahib. Always I saved the best fruit only for you."

Annie looked down at her hands as she took the bag from Suresh. "Go on, now. I'm sure you tell all the ladies that."

Suresh's protests faded as Annie walked away. She stepped over a pile of decaying vegetables, taking great care not to soil the shoes she'd purchased at Bata's a few days earlier. In spite of the stench, noise, ever-present flies, and press of the crowds, she had always looked forward to her weekly trip to Byculla's vegetable market. It gave her a reason to get away from her flat. Most days, she would walk to the market, about fifteen minutes each way. She enjoyed the exercise, even under the unforgiving scowl of the sun, as she braved the rubble, human waste, and other debris that turned the pavements into obstacle courses.

When she returned home, arms stiff from carrying her bags, she noticed the blinking red light on her answering machine. She still hadn't got used to the machine, a Christmas gift from Selwyn. She preferred the old days when people simply assumed you were out if you didn't answer the phone, and they called back later. She hated how her voice sounded on the machine as well. It reminded her of her niece, Karen, who had suffered from enlarged adenoids as a child.

After stocking the refrigerator with her purchases, Annie fixed a cup of tea and opened her last pack of Marie biscuits. Only after the tea had cooled so she could sip it comfortably did she press the play button on the machine.

"Annie, this is Ruby," the voice said. "The ladies are getting together tonight to plan the church raffle. I know you must have a thousand things to do before you move, but I hope you can join us. Give me a call, okay?"

Annie continued dunking her biscuit into the milky tea, clucking with annoyance as a piece broke off and sank to the bottom of the cup. She fished it out with her spoon. She had forgotten about the meeting, and although she was glad Ruby had called to remind her, for once she wanted just to stay home instead. Over the past few years, there were times when she wished she wasn't so involved with the church ladies, who always seemed to be buzzing with activity related to some committee or the other.

Then again, as Selwyn often told her, if it weren't for the many diversions offered by Gloria Church, she wouldn't have anything to do with her time. Of course, in a week, it wouldn't matter much. She wondered if Ruby or any of the others would still call her.

Annie deposited her cup in the sink and settled into her favorite armchair near the living-room window. She shuffled through the pile of magazines on the coffee table and fished out a month-old copy of *India Today*, which she hadn't finished reading even though she'd already swept the latest issue into the pile on the floor. Every month, the old jari puranawala would come to her door, inspect her collection of paper, bottles, and cans, and offer her a handful of coins in exchange. She wondered whether the street vendors whom she depended upon, trading everything from fresh fish to rock salt, would make their rounds through the buildings in Selwyn's gated community in Thana. She adjusted the glasses on her nose, began thumbing through her magazine, and soon drifted off to sleep.

The doorbell jolted Annie awake. A quick glance at the clock told her she'd slept for almost four hours. With a grunt, she heaved herself out of the pliant armchair and opened the door.

The baker greeted her and retrieved the customary loaf—still warm from the oven—from his wicker basket. Annie reminded him that it was her last order and set the loaf down on a plate in the kitchen. After a moment's hesitation, she covered it with gauze netting, denying the flies that strayed in from the open windows a fresh meal. Selwyn had told her about the new window screens many builders were installing now, but she hadn't bothered. Maybe the Menezes family would take care of it after they moved in. The younger generation expected these modern conveniences.

She hummed an old hymn as she bustled about the kitchen, wiping the countertops and putting away a few jars of spices that she'd left out the night before. It really was unlike her to leave things lying about, but she'd been so tired and had gone to bed immediately after eating dinner.

The yeasty aroma of fresh-baked bread called to Annie, as much as she tried to resist it. Before she knew it, she'd broken off a piece and stuffed it into her mouth. She thought about calling Ruby back.

Instead, she turned to the stereo cabinet, thankful that Selwyn had finally shown her how to use the turntable the year before—something else that had always been Clive's responsibility. She pried open the latch on the matte black record case that sat on the bottom shelf and flipped through the albums until she found the one she wanted, a compilation of movie themes performed by the James Last orchestra. She removed the shining black disk from its sleeve, holding it by the edges. After she placed it on the turntable and set the arm into motion, she adjusted the volume on the amplifier, flooding the room with sound. She closed her eyes and began to sway to the music. She could almost feel Clive's arms guiding her, as he had done so many times over the course of their lives together.

Clive had been the one to sign them up for ballroom dancing lessons at the Catholic Gymkhana, a year after they were married. Annie, terrified at first of making a fool of herself, soon found herself enjoying the lessons and looking forward to them each week. Of course, things changed a little after she gave birth to Selwyn, Joan, and Maria in rapid succession, before the hysterectomy that put a premature end to her childbearing years. When Selwyn grew old enough to take care of his siblings, Annie and Clive returned to the Gymkhana and even took part in competitions. She remembered how Clive's chest puffed out while he gazed at the diminutive silver awards that occupied prime position in their showcase.

She opened her eyes and looked at the showcase now, dreading the task of packing its contents. The hand-carved mahogany frame remained unscratched, and the glass door shone as brightly as they had when Annie and Clive got married. Three shelves held a collection of trophies and plaques that belonged to Selwyn and Joan, with a sprinkling of medals signifying Maria's contribution. The top shelf, however, was reserved for her and Clive. In the center, Annie had placed Clive's mortuary card.

After all this time, his picture still brought a hint of moisture to her eyes.

The needle skipped on the record, jarring her back to the present, and she moved the arm to the next track. The new owners would inherit the stereo as well, but the record case—all that was left of Clive's music collection—would be entrusted to the care of the movers in a few days. Selwyn had promised they would take especially good care of it.

The music resumed, and Annie settled back into her armchair. Once again, she closed her eyes, letting the melody wash over her like the monsoon rain that cleansed the city of its dust and grime. When the needle reached the end of the record and glided back to its resting position, she stood up, stretched, and shuffled to the telephone. She stifled a sigh of relief when she heard the recording on the other end.

"Hello, Ruby. This is Annie calling you back. I'm sorry, but I don't feel too well today. I'll have to miss the meeting tonight. I'll call you tomorrow. Bye."

After she replaced the receiver, Annie raised her head and peered through the iron grille that covered the window. Storm clouds had been gathering all afternoon, transforming the sky from a uniform, misty gray to angry charcoal. Annie inhaled, savoring the comforting scent of damp earth that foretold the rain. A crack of thunder made her jump, and moments later, the skies burst open. Sheets of water pounded on the concrete walls of the building, sounding like a load of gravel being dumped from a truck.

Within minutes, flies covered the kitchen table, seeking refuge from the downpour. Annie rummaged under the sink for a packet of bait. As she drizzled the crystals of sugar, coated with bright red poison, onto a saucer, she remembered how Clive always sprinkled a few drops of water over it. It helped attract the flies faster, he'd said.

He was good at taking care of little things like that, especially in the early days when they'd moved into the flat and didn't have enough money to hire a servant. They'd divided up the household duties, Clive doing the cleaning and running most of the errands while she saw to the cooking and laundry. When Selwyn was born, they'd finally hired a servant who helped Annie on weekdays. Although Clive was spending more time at work, he had a schedule of tasks he would run through each weekend. Annie smiled as she recalled how organized he'd been, making a list every Friday night and checking off each item as he completed it. She knew how much he had hated the flies during the monsoon, grumbling as he cleaned up the mess each night.

Now the flies buzzed around the table, spinning in tight circles on their backs as the poison took hold. Annie walked back to the window and once again breathed in the heavy, moisture-laden air. She still loved the rain, even when it clogged the gutters and flooded the streets. Most of all, she exhilarated in the brief respite it provided from the oppressive heat.

She opened the refrigerator and began to gather the ingredients for dinner—plump, green tendlis the size of her thumb, and juicy, red tomatoes. On occasion, she had stuffed the shelves to capacity and had to ask the neighbors to store some food, just for a day. She had enjoyed those dinner parties, even though she had so much to do. The last one she'd planned was for Clive's retirement.

The day had finally come, a few months after Clive's sixtieth birthday. The company honored Clive and seven other retirees at its annual celebration held at the Willingdon Club that year. Annie had prepared for this day for some time, and she looked forward to spending more time with Clive. Yet she wondered how he'd cope with the change. Some of their friends spent their retirement traveling, but Clive had never enjoyed seeing the world—or even the rest of India. He hated trains, refused to get on an airplane, and buses made him ill.

After the three-hour function ended and Clive managed to extricate himself from the throng of well-wishers, they hailed two taxis. They packed the children into the first and settled into the second.

"I'm glad that's over," Clive whispered. "Tomorrow, I can relax. Then I'm going to start doing some work on the flat. We need to paint the bedroom, so why not do the entire flat?"

"Will you get everything done before the party?" she said. "We have only a week."

"Don't worry," he said. "That's plenty of time."

And, true to his word, he finished painting the day before. The flat sparkled and smelled like linseed oil, which Annie didn't entirely mind. She just hoped their guests wouldn't mind, either.

They spent the afternoon setting up furniture, pilfering chairs from every room in the flat and arranging them around the perimeter of the living room. In one corner, they placed the dining table, which would soon be filled with glasses, ice buckets, and an assortment of liquor. Clive's favorite, a bottle of well-aged single-malt Chivas Regal, took pride of place. He refused to drink the so-called IMFL—Indian-made foreign liquor—that some of his friends swore tasted just like the imports. He claimed he could always spot the impostors, and Annie never had reason to doubt him. She never shared Clive's taste for Scotch, preferring an occasional glass of wine instead.

That day, Annie ruled the kitchen, with Selwyn and Joan serving as sous chefs. They had all the prep work done and the main courses simmering on the stove when the first guests arrived. Clive's favorite—vegetable pulao, tinted a pale yellow with turmeric and topped with a liberal sprinkling of golden raisins and cashews—anchored the menu. Other dishes included a selection from Annie's family recipes, handed down over generations: fried pomfret, breaded potato cutlets, a fiery chicken vindaloo, and delicately flavored egg curry.

The guests started arriving by six that evening—Clive's family and Annie's, adults and children. As the adults took their seats and Clive fulfilled beverage requests, Maria passed around bowls of salted cashews, chivda, and spicy peanuts. Annie and Joan continued working in the kitchen, taking occasional breaks to venture into the living room and join briefly in the increasingly loud conversations that zipped back and forth like bullets while the guests nursed their drinks and smoked their cigarettes. Meanwhile, Selwyn and Maria kept the younger children diverted and—for the most part—out of the way, in the largest of the three bedrooms.

Finally, after Joan had cleared the table of the clutter generated by Clive's bar-tending duties, Annie helped her carry out steaming dishes and arrange them buffet-style, together with bowls of home-made chili pickle and mango chutney. One of the contingent of priests from Gloria Church, always invited on these occasions, stood to say grace and the room fell silent at once. As soon as the chorus of amens faded, the guests converged on the dinner table like jackals over the carcass of a fallen antelope.

After several trips to the kitchen to refill dishes and ensure the children were getting their share from the pots and pans scattered about the stovetop and counters, Annie sat down with her plate. She enjoyed the brief respite, fielding compliments on the food, before it was time for dessert.

Several hours later, after hailing a taxi for the last guest, Clive collected dirty dishes and transported them to the sink, Selwyn emptied ashtrays, and Joan helped Maria rearrange the furniture. While Clive washed the dishes, Annie put the leftovers away after she'd sent the children off to bed. This was her favorite time, just the two of them in the kitchen, sifting through the best of the gossip and retelling some of the stories for each other's benefit.

Less than a month later, she had sat by Clive's paralyzed body at Jaslok Hospital, struggling to comprehend the neurologist's well-meaning but increasingly despondent reports.

*

The day before the movers arrived, Annie tackled her final task: the old Godrej steel cupboard in her bedroom. She rummaged through the first shelf, sorting out clothes she hadn't worn for years. Maybe she should just donate them to the church. She didn't really need much, after all, and she wouldn't have a lot of room at Selwyn's flat.

After she created four neat piles of clothing on her bed, she turned her attention to the next shelf. She reached behind another heap of clothes, and her fingers brushed against cold metal. Frowning, she closed her fingers around the object and retrieved it—a tarnished silver frame that held a faded, monochrome photograph. She wiped it carefully with her sleeve. In the picture, Selwyn and Ritu smiled at her from under an archway of flowers. Annie sat on the edge of her bed, clutching the frame to her chest. She knew why she'd tucked that picture away.

Selwyn had resisted all their attempts to arrange a marriage. Annie had pleaded with him to meet the girls—nice Goan girls—that she'd lined up, with the full cooperation of their parents. Clive stayed out of it for the most part. Perhaps, Annie realized, he knew that Selwyn's stubborn streak would manifest itself.

When Selwyn finally introduced Ritu to them and announced they'd been dating for over a year, the news devastated Annie. Why hadn't he told her before? Marrying a Mangalorean girl! That was completely inexcusable.

Annie begged Clive to intervene, but he simply laughed and shrugged his shoulders. "What are you going to do, Annie?"

he said. "Forbid them to get married? He's twenty-six. Old enough to do what he wants."

Six months later, Selwyn and Ritu were married at Gloria Church, with most of Annie's friends in attendance at the Mass. She noticed a few of them nudging each other as they waited for the priest. She held her head high and pretended to be absorbed in the flower arrangements. The bright reds and luminous yellows softened the stark whiteness of the marble altar.

She couldn't bring herself to display the wedding photographs anywhere in the flat. It took almost six months for the last of her misgivings to melt away. Finally, at Clive's urging, she accepted her new daughter-in-law into the family. Over time, she grew close to Ritu, even favoring her over Joan's husband, who happened to be a good, church-going Goan boy. Annie's wish to see all her children married, however, had not yet been fulfilled. Maria, to Annie's consternation and bitter disappointment, had remained resolutely single.

Turning back to the cupboard, Annie continued to ferry piles of clothing to the bed. On the last shelf, she discovered a bundle of candles, still in their protective cellophane wrap. With a silent prayer of thanks, she picked out two of them.

She placed the candles in brass holders at the base of the giant, pyramidal statue of the Infant Jesus of Prague that looked down from the altar above the showcase. Soon, the statue would be on its way to Thana, so the discovery of the candles had presented her with a divine opportunity. As she muttered the prayers she'd recited a thousand times before, she realized how dirty the statue had become. A thin, hazy layer of soot and grease coated the entire ceramic figure but was most noticeable on the pale, cherubic face that gazed at her from under a golden crown. The blue eyes had lost their sparkle, and dust covered the tip of the scepter that the child held in his right hand.

She had brought the statue home after her first trip to the famous shrine at Nasik, almost ten years earlier. After a day's train journey in the oppressive heat and a walk that left her feet crying out for relief, she fought her way through the crowds of sweaty devotees, nearly overcome by the smell of stale urine and horse manure that emanated from the muddy streets. As she left the shrine with Clive, she spotted a vendor selling an assortment of statues arranged on a folding table that groaned under its burden. Clive laughed when she suggested buying the largest one, until he realized she was serious. After a feeble protest, he assented and carried the statue—easily half his height—all the way back to the bus depot and then on the train. The children had teased her mercilessly when she'd arrived home. Later, she had cajoled Clive into building the altar.

She looked up at the statue now. The infant's eyes seemed to bore into her soul, sensing the tumult that churned within. After she extinguished the candles, she took a damp rag from the kitchen and began to clean the statue, starting at the base. She wished the children were still together to tease her once again.

"We're here, ma," Selwyn said. Annie opened her eyes as they passed through a large stone archway that signaled the entrance to Rainbow Gardens. They drove past an immaculate garden that surrounded a swimming pool. Annie cast a longing gaze at a few limestone cottages with clay tile roofs and landscaped yards, before they turned onto a road lined with towering high-rise developments. She recognized the bland, tan and white, twenty-story building even before she could read the sign. Selwyn escorted her from the car, retrieved her suitcase, and thanked Vijay, politely declining his offer to take memsahib on a tour of the city.

Annie clung to Selwyn's arm as they walked across the lobby, tiled in gray and pink marble, toward the lift. The fresh, almost antiseptic surroundings contrasted sharply with her old flat building on Clare Road. When Selwyn had moved his family into the flat the year before, to be closer to his and Ritu's jobs, he'd told Annie that many of Thana's suburban neighborhoods had been developed within the last fifteen or twenty years. The developers, armed with large sums of black money, completed projects in record time after they'd paid off the local government officials. Demand for housing far exceeded supply—all the flats in Selwyn's building had sold out long before construction had even started.

Selwyn hummed a tune from one of the latest Bollywood movies—a taste Annie never shared, as much as she'd tried—as they ascended to the twelfth floor.

Ritu rushed out of the flat as soon as Annie stepped out of the lift, followed by the children. They gathered around Annie in the hallway, showering her with kisses. She bent to kiss Dominic, asleep in Ritu's arms. His older brother looked up at Annie with large brown eyes. "Welcome home, granny," he said as he grabbed her hand and led her into the flat.

Annie glanced over her shoulder at Selwyn, whose attention was focused on the sleeping infant. "Yes," she said, wiping her eyes with the back of her hand. "This is home, now."

Retribution

S ACHIN AWOKE WITH A start to the sound of fists pounding on the door of his flat. "Hurry up, Sachin," a voice called from the hallway. "Your shop has been looted!"

He leaped up from the bed as Sujata stirred next to him. "You stay here with the children," he said. She stared at him, bleary-eyed. "I'm going downstairs."

He found Major Kulkarni waiting outside the door, clutching a handgun. They raced down the stairs and along the narrow alley toward the shops at the back of the L-shaped building.

"I heard a noise from my flat," the major said. "I ran out to check and thought I saw some men near your shop. I shouted at them, and they ran away. I followed them into the road, but they had a car waiting—"

"The watchman?" Sachin's breath came in short, sharp bursts.

The major shook his head. "Drunk, as usual. I found him passed out in his chair."

As they reached the back entrance to the shop, the major tensed and tightened his grip on the gun. The door that led into Sachin's stockroom hung at an odd angle on its hinges. Jagged splinters poked out around the handle, and the padlock that secured the solitary latch lay on the floor.

The heavy, oily smell of kerosene filled Sachin's lungs, and he put a hand over his nose. The major sniffed the air and frowned. "I must have stopped them just in time."

Sachin looked around the stockroom, his eyes capturing snapshots of the damage but his mind refusing to process the images. Broken glass littered the concrete floor. Most of his carefully stocked shelves lay bare. In one corner, a sack of charcoal had been slashed open, its contents scattered around the room like enormous rat droppings. As he entered the shop, he saw that the front counter had been smashed in. A few items—bags of colorful sweets, shiny foil packets of supari, school notebooks, pencils and pens—were piled in a heap on the floor next to a stack of newspapers soaked in kerosene.

"Who would do this?" the major asked. "This was not just a random act. None of the other shops have been touched."

Sachin turned to him, a wild look in his eyes. "Damodar," he said through clenched teeth. "It has to be Damodar."

"Do you want me to call the police?"

Sachin's breathing grew labored. "No," he said, after surveying the destruction one more time. "They won't help. Damodar has them all in his pocket."

The major placed a hand on Sachin's shoulder as they walked back through the stockroom. "Just let me know how I can help."

When Sachin returned to bed, he found Sujata asleep, her snores marking a gentle rhythm as her chest rose and fell. He thought about waking her but decided against it. He paced around the bedroom for a while before realizing that sleep would probably elude him. Although it was still dark out, he heard the familiar, growing buzz of the city stirring. He walked back to his shop, past the night watchman still slumped in his chair.

He picked up his red ledger and removed the pencil behind his ear as he began to check his inventory. He wished Sujata could help him with this task, as she normally did.

Several hours later, he trudged upstairs with the ledger tucked under one arm. Sujata opened her mouth as he walked in, but his expression silenced her at once. The children ran to him. They hugged his legs and giggled, quite unaware that the world had just fallen apart around them. Sachin collapsed in the middle of the floor, and Mukul climbed into his lap. Shalini—although just a year older than Mukul—had already, at the age of four, grown to regard such displays of affection as too undignified. She stood to one side, arms crossed, until Sujata took her into her arms, deaf to her cries of protest. Together, they watched as Sachin hugged Mukul close to his chest. Sachin closed his eyes and rocked on the cold stone floor.

The shop remained closed for over two weeks. By the time it reopened, Sachin had cleaned out the meager savings they'd accumulated over the years, and he'd managed to restock only a few shelves. At first, he was sure sales would pick up, and that he could build the rest of his inventory over time. As the days went by, however, he began to realize the magnitude of the challenge facing him.

"What is this, Sachin?" a customer asked as he waited at the counter. Dinesh Trivedi worked at the Sales Tax office down the road and often stopped by Sachin's shop before taking the bus home. "I used to come to you every week, and you had no problem getting these things for me. Toys and chocolate for the children, cigarettes for me, soap, cleaning supplies, paper clips...these are not rare and precious items, no? But now you say you cannot help me?"

Sachin hung his head. "Please, Trivedi sahib, just a few days. Come back soon, and I will have everything you need."

But Trivedi sahib did not come back, and many other customers followed suit. As Sachin feared, they had started visiting Damodar's much larger provision store that had opened a year earlier, less than a kilometer away on Dockyard Road. Even during the busiest time, right after the Sales Tax offices closed, he had only a handful of customers. Before the incident, Sachin would keep the shop open until ten, when the evening's stream of customers would finally trickle to a few young men who came for cigarettes or just a box of matches. Now, the shop was deserted by six.

"What are we going to do?" Sujata asked him that night as they finished a hurried meal of lentils and rice. "We're not making any money, and nothing will change until you can restock your supply. Can't you persuade the vendors to let you have items on credit?"

Sachin looked into her eyes, filled with a dark, brooding desperation, and his heart sank. He struggled to summon his confidence—if he gave into what he was feeling, he feared the fragile threads that held Sujata's spirit together would fray completely.

"Don't worry," he said, forcing a smile. "I'll find a way to restock the shop. Once we do that, I'm sure our regular customers will come back."

"What about the rent?" she continued. "Bhasin sahib will be here tomorrow, and we have nothing to give him."

On the first day of each month, the building's landlord came to collect the rent. Sachin paid on time, maintaining a cordial—if not warm—relationship with Bhasin sahib. Although Sachin thought the combined rent for the shop and their flat seemed a little steep, he accepted their arrangement and never once thought about moving to a cheaper location. Bhasin sahib was polite and respectful with his tenants, and sometimes, he'd stop to accept a glass of tea and chat for a few minutes. In those fleeting moments, Sachin felt honored that Bhasin sahib considered him an equal, sharing the common bond of their respective trades.

Sachin pushed his bowl away and walked over to Sujata. He put a hand on her shoulder, and stroked the lustrous hair that fell almost to her waist, set free from the braids that she normally wore during the day. "Don't worry," he said again. "I'll talk to him. With everything that has happened here, I'm sure he wouldn't mind waiting a few days longer."

When Bhasin sahib arrived the next morning, Sujata persuaded him to sit down for some tea. He lowered his considerable bulk into the single folding chair reserved for guests. He made it look like a toy, something in a doll house, and it creaked as he shifted his weight. While Sachin engaged their guest in conversation, Sujata hovered in the background with the children clinging to the folds of her sari. Although Bhasin sahib wore an expression of placid amiability while they discussed the upcoming elections, Sachin hesitated before making his plea.

"Bhasin sahib," he said, twisting the hem of his kurta with one hand, "I'm afraid I don't have the rent money today. I'll have it in a few days."

Bhasin sahib's brow creased into a frown. Sachin noticed the thin sheen of sweat on his forehead. Perhaps the tea was too hot. Sachin waited for a response but, getting none, continued. "You see…the damage to the shop has caused many losses. I am trying very hard to build up my sales again, but it will take time—" He spread his hands, avoiding Sujata's eyes.

The big man lifted the glass of tea, then poured some of it into the saucer in his other hand. He blew on the saucer and poured the tea back into the glass. Still, he remained silent.

Sachin struggled to suppress the trembling in his hands and legs, which refused to obey him. Bhasin sahib, his face devoid of emotion, raised the glass and took a long sip of tea. Then he put the glass back on the saucer, cradling it in one massive hand. He wiped his lips with the other and, at last, he spoke.

"Sachin, we have known each other now for over ten years. You are a good tenant. I have heard from others in this building that you helped them when they had problems, that you have given them food when they had none, that you and your wife invite their children into your home and care for them." He handed the glass and saucer to Sujata, who disentangled herself from the children and carried it into the kitchen.

"During all this time, I can remember only one occasion when you did not pay the rent on the day I came to collect it."

He stood up slowly, his belly protruding as his body unfolded to its full height. He straightened his gray jacket and smoothed the folds of his pristine white dhoti. It glowed in the sunlight filtering in through the single, small window set high in the back wall. "I will give you one more week. Make sure to have it then, and I will not charge you a penalty."

Sachin cried out in relief and bent low to clasp the big man's feet. "Thank you, Bhasin sahib. Thank you very much. I will have the money for you a week from today. I will not fail."

Bhasin sahib waved his hands in dismissal. "Make sure that you do," he said, as he lumbered toward the door.

After Bhasin sahib had left, Sachin reassured Sujata that he would find a way to get the money. They spent over an hour coming up with increasingly improbable schemes to turn the business around.

"Maybe we should just sell the shop and leave this place," Sujata said, when they were too exhausted to discuss the issue any more. Sachin looked at her and ran his tongue over his parched lips but said nothing. He wasn't going to give up, not after everything they had been through.

A few days later, Sachin arrived at the office of Govind Lala, the moneylender. The office, a single room with unadorned, whitewashed walls, lay nestled in between vendors of stainless steel cookware off Carnac Road, near the bustling Crawford Market. The briny odor of fish from the market drifted down the narrow street, flooding the office in spite of the ceiling fan that creaked through its ponderous rotations overhead. Sachin wrinkled his nose while he waited for Govind Lala to arrive. He sat in a stiff-backed, padded wooden chair in front of a slate-colored steel desk piled with stacks of papers.

In one corner, a solitary black telephone broke the sea of whiteness. Sachin eyed it with apprehension, expecting it to ring at any moment.

Sachin had heard of the moneylenders who carried on a thriving business in various parts of Bombay, but he had never dared to do business with them before. Vivek—one of the building's residents—had told him about Govind Lala. A year earlier, Vivek himself took a loan from Govind Lala when he lost his job as a driver for a family in a swanky Malabar Hill bungalow. "It is not cheap," he said. "They will charge you a huge amount of interest. But what can you do when you have nowhere else to go?" Sachin took down the address. Something told him not to mention it to Sujata just yet. Then he caught the number 3 BEST bus that stopped close to his shop, which took him to Crawford Market. A few inquiries had sufficed to direct him to Govind Lala's office.

A door in the back of the room opened, and a thin, tall man walked in. He wore a Western-style jacket and navy polyester trousers. Under the jacket, Sachin saw a shirt the color of the royal blue ink he used in his fountain pen. The top three buttons were open, revealing a thick mat of curly hair amid which nestled a pendant that dangled from a gold chain around Govind Lala's long neck. He bobbed his head, reminding Sachin of the chickens that squawked and scratched about in the open expanse of dirt behind his shop.

Sachin rose, hands clasped, and bowed. Govind Lala nodded again and gestured to the chair. The transaction took place with surprising speed as Govind Lala appeared in a hurry to get to a business meeting. He recorded the amount of the loan in a thick ledger not unlike the one Sachin used for his shop. The payment terms were disclosed on a single sheet of paper that Sachin signed with a shaky hand. Then Govind Lala turned back toward the door and shouted something in Marathi. A short while later, a servant shuffled into the room, carrying the cash in a brown paper bag.

Sachin thought about counting it but feared that doing so would earn him Govind Lala's disfavor, so he merely bowed again. He left, clutching the bag with both hands. This time, he allowed himself the luxury of a taxi ride back home. It would be foolish, he thought, to entrust his fate to the overcrowded BEST buses where nimble fingers were known to make short work of a passenger's belongings.

When the time came for Bhasin sahib to collect the overdue rent, Sachin told Sujata about the loan. At first, she railed at him, fists clenched. Then she broke down and lamented their fate for several minutes while Sachin massaged his aching temples. She calmed down only after he sat with her on the edge of their bed, one arm around her shoulders, and promised that he would not borrow any more money from Govind Lala. After all, once the customers returned, he'd be able to pay off the loan and interest. Everything would be the way it was.

But the customers did not return. Another month went by, another rent payment came due, and still business was slow. Sachin couldn't understand it. His shop offered the one-stop convenience of purchasing everyday items, but few of his regular customers came by. Even the schoolchildren, who used to purchase chewing gum and sweets, counting out a handful of coins each time, had all but vanished.

He even painted a new sign above the shop that read, in bold blue letters on a white background: Patel's General Stores.

Underneath, he repeated the words in Hindi. As he surveyed his work, a thought struck him. Perhaps he needed to add more items to his shop. But to do that, he needed more money.

Once more, Sachin made a trip to Crawford Market, and Govind Lala advanced him another sum, equal to the first. He warned Sachin that his first installment was coming due, and this was the last loan he would receive if he did not pay on time. Sachin bowed his head, reassuring Govind Lala that he would not be late.

That week, Sachin increased his inventory, adding trendy items like the latest women's cosmetics, imported cigarettes, and the little Japanese electronic toys that were becoming all the rage among Bombay's affluent children. He even expanded his network of suppliers, going to great lengths to acquire these items at the best wholesale prices. But none of it seemed to make a difference. When Sunday night arrived and he finished his accounting, sales were almost the same as they had been the previous week.

As Sachin lay awake, he thought maybe Sujata was right after all. Maybe they should just sell the shop and move away from Bombay. Maybe he could find a job and forget about this wretched shop and the growing mountain of debt it had brought him. Then he remembered how his father had left him the shop before he'd died. When Sachin was twelve, he'd started helping out at the shop after school. "Someday," his father had said, "this shop will be yours, son. Promise me you will always deal honestly with your customers." Sachin, both excited and terrified at the prospect of running the shop all by himself, had promised.

*

The word spread around the building that the Patels were having financial difficulties. One by one, residents came to visit, offering to help in whatever manner they could. Mrs. Pathak, the elderly widow who lived alone on the fourth floor, gave them a bag of rice. She had too much, she said, and Sachin would be doing her a favor by using it before the grain moths got it all. Brian Fernandes, the tenth-standard student who attended St. Magnus, brought an assortment of Goan sweets— bebinca pudding, guava cheese, and coconut pancakes. It was left over from a birthday party, he said, and they simply couldn't eat any more. The young, childless Marwari couple from the flat above came by with a few toys. Their parents had showered them with toys after their wedding, they said, but what use were toys if they didn't have any children?

Sachin and Sujata thanked them profusely after futile attempts to refuse their neighbors' generosity. They knew each of their benefactors' circumstances—most of them couldn't really afford to be generous. At last, when Sachin began to turn them away, they started to show up at his shop, buying small trinkets and food items that he knew they would not normally purchase. As he remonstrated with them, they told him not to worry. "You helped us so many times before," Major Kulkarni said. "Now let us help you."

When the day came to make his first payment to Govind Lala, Sachin found himself short by over ten thousand rupees. And he had nothing left for the rent that was due in a few days. He arrived, shivering, at the sweltering office with a plastic shopping bag clutched to his chest.

Govind Lala frowned as his servant counted the money and whispered in his ear. "This is not the right amount, Sachin," he said. "You are missing ten thousand, five hundred, and fifty rupees."

Sachin studied a spot on the floor, not daring to look at Govind Lala. "Please, sahib," he whispered, "just a few days more. I will have the rest for you soon, I promise."

Silence fell over the small room. Govind Lala stood up, scraping the metal legs of his chair against the floor with a horrible screech that made Sachin's skin crawl.

"Look at me, Sachin," he said in a calm, even voice. It made Sachin wish he were invisible. He wanted to run away that instant, but his legs felt as if he were knee-deep in thick, oozing mud. At length, he raised his eyes to meet Govind Lala's unwavering stare.

"Please, sahib," he whispered again, having nothing else to say.

"Sachin," Govind Lala spread his hands, "do you think I am a successful businessman?"

"Yes, sahib. Very much so."

"And I have become successful, Sachin, by hard work, not by charity. If I make allowances for one of my customers, I will have to make allowances for all of them. And what then? I lose money, and I cannot serve my customers."

Sachin did not feel a response was warranted, so he said nothing. He lowered his head once more to escape the cold fire he saw in the other man's eyes.

Govind Lala sighed. "You are young," he said, "and so perhaps you cannot fully understand the nature of a business transaction. Yet you are a businessman like me, aren't you? You own a paan shop or something?"

Sachin willed himself to speak. "General stores, sahib."

"And what would happen, Sachin, if your customers bought items but did not pay? If they kept promising to settle accounts later? Would your business survive for long?"

Sachin thought of old Mrs. Pathak, to whom he had often extended credit because her rent ate up most of her meager government pension. He had not given it a second thought at the time, but clearly Govind Lala was telling him never to indulge in such a weakness.

"No, sahib," he said, folding his hands.

"I will send one of my men on Friday," Govind Lala said, the steel in his voice cutting through Sachin like a butcher's knife. "Three days from now. You will submit the remaining payment, plus another two thousand rupees as a late fee. Twelve thousand, five hundred and fifty rupees, to be paid in full. Is that clear?"

"Yes, sahib. Thank you, sahib." Sachin backed out of the room until he was near the door, then turned and fled into the bustling street.

He spent the rest of the morning on the phone, trying to arrange returns of some of his merchandise. Most of the vendors agreed, after considerable haggling, to receive the returned items for a product credit only, and at considerably less than the price Sachin had paid. None were able to give him cash. After a few more calls that resulted in the same response, he abandoned his efforts.

While Sujata and the children spent the afternoon at Victoria Gardens, Sachin paced around the stockroom, trying to come up with fresh ideas to raise money. For a moment, he even considered selling the shop, as Sujata had wanted, but how would he find a buyer in two days?

As he sat at the wooden shelf that served as a desk, sipping tea, his eye caught an advertisement in the daily newspaper. That was it! He would offer a closing sale, marking down every item in the store so that it would sell quickly. He could tell his customers he was leaving Bombay, just as Sujata had wanted. Once he had paid Govind Lala, he could change his plans and keep the shop open.

Would he be able to include Sujata in the deception? For a few hours, he fussed around the stockroom, arranging and rearranging the contents of shelves, dreading the time when Sujata and the children would return.

Finally, he retrieved a dusty slate and some colored chalk from a steel cupboard. He made a simple sign that read, "Closing Sale! Everything at Reduced Price!" and propped it on the front counter. Next door, the owner of the paan and cigarette shop craned his head around the counter to read it. He told Sachin he hoped it would drive more customers to his shop, for that would benefit both of them.

When Sujata returned with the children, they clamored around him, full of stories about riding the majestic elephants, the monkeys who scowled at them, the lions who scared them, and all the other sights that had enchanted them that afternoon. Sujata gave Sachin a strange look, but she did not seem to be in a talkative mood.

As soon as they had put the children to bed, she drew him aside and demanded to know what was going on. He told her the story he had woven with such dexterity that he almost believed it himself. She had been right, he said—the only choice left was to sell the shop. He had found some interested buyers, but first he had to reduce his inventory. Her eyes brightened as he described his plans for the sale. He hoped to be done with everything in a month, so they should start making plans to move. Sujata had always wanted to return to the place of her birth, a small industrial town about a hundred kilometers north of Bombay where her parents still lived. She was certain Sachin could find some work there, and they could stay with her parents until they were settled.

For a moment, her face clouded as she told him how she remembered his father's sacrifice and what the shop had meant to him. But she embraced Sachin, clinging to him with a fervor that surprised him. It reminded him of when they were newlyweds, before the children. He began to wonder if he should carry out his plan after all, for he knew she would never forgive him when she discovered the truth.

The next morning, several people passing Sachin's shop on their way to work stopped to read his sign. A few of them chatted with him and made small purchases, lifting his spirits. As the day wore on, more came by, including many of the building's residents. Soon, the whole community heard the news: the Patels were closing down the shop and moving.

By the time Sachin lowered the shutters, he estimated that the traffic to his store had almost doubled. But after he counted the day's receipts, his heart sank. The two-day total came to around five thousand rupees, better than he had done for a while, but a long way from the twelve thousand he needed.

Sachin's restlessness that night woke Sujata an hour after they had gone to bed. She put an arm around his waist, murmuring that everything would be okay. She would send a telegram to her parents the next day to let them know of their plans. "Soon," she said, "this will all be over, and we will have a fresh start." At these words, Sachin grew even more troubled. As soon as Sujata fell asleep again, he got out of bed, being careful not to wake her. He sat on the floor for a while, watching her sleep, marveling at how peaceful she looked.

It reminded him of how calm she had been at their wedding, only the second time they had met. The first was when they were children and their parents had arranged the marriage. Near the end of the multiple-day celebration, he had found it hard to focus as they gathered in the mandap, with the priest chanting in Sanskrit and the sweet smell of incense overwhelming his senses. He clutched his garland so tight that he crushed some of the flowers, as he waited until the moment when the curtain separating him from his bride would be opened. He kept his eyes lowered as the priest continued. Then the time came. As he reached over to Sujata and placed the garland around her neck, she looked into his eyes and smiled. Like a ray of light piercing the monsoon clouds, that look had dissolved away all his fears and doubts in a single, fleeting moment of clarity.

He wished he had that clarity now.

By Thursday night, Sachin still needed over four thousand rupees. Throughout the day, he had kept hoping for just one more customer who would make a large purchase, but each transaction only served as a reminder of how far he was from his goal. Panic numbed his senses to the point where he went through the rest of the evening not even knowing—or caring— what the next day would bring. Before sleep claimed him, he made up his mind. He would keep his promise to Sujata, even if it meant letting his father down. He would sell the shop, and they could move away from Bombay as she wanted—away from the ashes of failure—to start a new life together.

A hazy dawn cast diffuse shadows in the kitchen as Sachin began to prepare tea. A loud hammering on the door made him jump, and he nearly knocked the battered aluminum pot off the stove. He opened the door a crack, but it was shoved in his face and three men burst in. The first was a heavy-set man with a dark, pock-marked complexion and thinning hair. He wore a white undershirt that accentuated his large paunch, below which a leather belt secured his faded denim jeans. The other two wore simple kurta-pajamas. Unlike the first man, they looked to be younger and in better physical condition.

"You are Sachin Patel?" the heavy man said, in accented Hindi.

Sachin nodded, unable to speak. The younger men took up positions behind Sachin and stood there without saying anything, their muscular arms crossed, eyes expressionless. He tore his gaze away from them and turned back to the older man.

"I'm Mr. Lobo," the man continued, before switching to English. "We work for Mr. Govind Lala, and we've come to collect the money that you owe." He cleared his throat. "Twelve thousand, five hundred and fifty rupees, including the late charge. Give me the money now."

Sachin's shoulders slumped. He walked back into the bedroom and reached under the bed, being careful not to wake Sujata. As he emerged, he peered into the children's room to make sure they were still asleep. He shut the door.

"Take it," he said, handing a crimson Lipton tea tin to Lobo. The lid rattled in his unsteady hands. "This is everything we have."

The other men stepped forward, but Lobo waved them away. "Have patience, you bleddy buggers," he said. "Let me count it first."

Sachin watched, his heart sinking into his sandals, as Lobo emptied the contents of the tin onto the narrow counter near the stove. He arranged the notes into small piles, then started to count each one, dropping it back into the tin when he was done. As he did so, he scribbled on a scrap of paper that he fished out of a pocket in his jeans.

After counting the last pile, Lobo wrote some more on the paper, checked his numbers again, and looked up at Sachin.

"This isn't enough," he said. "Come on, men. What are you doing? Trying to cheat me?"

A sudden bout of nausea seized Sachin as he lurched forward. "Please, Lobo sahib. It is all we have. If I could just have some more time—"

"Shut up!" Lobo yelled, smashing his fist on the countertop. "Govind Lala does not make special deals for anyone, you bleddy bashturd!"

Sachin's legs gave way, and he sank to the floor. At a signal from Lobo, one of the men came forward and slapped him, the blow searing his cheek like a hot iron. He heard a soft cry, and turned to see Sujata standing behind him, her eyes wide.

The man who had struck him noticed her, too, and clapped a burly hand over her mouth. As she struggled, he pinned her wrists behind her with his other hand.

"Please," Sachin said, tears stinging his eyes. "Leave her alone. This is my fault."

A toothy grin spread across Lobo's face. He barked an order to the men, and one of them gagged Sujata with a faded yellow rag while the other continued to restrain her. She had stopped struggling and her body had gone limp. Sachin avoided her eyes.

Lobo turned his attention back to Sachin. "You have kids?" Sachin stole a quick glance at the closed door.

"Please," Sachin repeated, lowering his voice, "don't hurt them. It is all my fault."

Lobo gestured at one of the men, who moved over to the door. His belly jiggled as he began to roar with laughter. "What kind of bleddy goondas do you think we are, men?" he said. "We don't hurt kids. We have our honor, after all."

He pointed at the tin on the counter. "You see what a difficult situation you've created for me, Sachin? You didn't keep your part of the deal, men. I could order these buggers to teach you a real lesson, but how would you earn the money if you couldn't work?"

Out of the corner of his eye, Sachin observed Sujata's face, drained of color. He looked away, unable to face the emptiness in her eyes.

Lobo shouted some more orders to the man who held Sujata. The two of them gagged Sachin as well, then tied his feet together and his hands behind his back. Lobo kicked his knees, and Sachin collapsed on the floor. A diffuse pain began to spread through his chest. As Lobo stood above him, Sachin closed his eyes, but the expected blow never came. Instead, Lobo bent close enough that Sachin could smell the pungent odor of feni on his breath. "I still need to teach you a lesson," he said, "so you never forget what Govind Lala has told you."

He turned away, and Sachin watched with helpless frustration as Lobo dragged Sujata into the bedroom. The man near Sachin smiled at him, exposing yellowed, uneven teeth.

Sachin wriggled on the floor, trying to sit up, but his captor kicked him in his ribs. He fell back again as the pain knifed through him. He heard the sharp sound of fabric tearing. Sujata's muffled scream sounded like it was coming from very far away. Then he heard Lobo swearing in Konkani, and a cold rage began to replace his fear. Once more, he fought against his bonds, but the man who stood over him had done his job well.

The erratic thumping of the bed filled Sachin's ears as he lay on the floor, hot tears burning a path down his cheeks. The man placed a heavy foot on his chest, pinning him down. Sachin's scream emerged as a subdued whimper, like a puppy separated from its mother. He fought the bile rising in his throat, realizing he would choke on his own vomit if he gave in. After an eternity, Lobo emerged from the bedroom, his greasy hair slightly disheveled and his undershirt stained with sweat. He grinned at Sachin and picked up the tin of cash from the kitchen counter. The three men left without saying a word to Sachin.

Ever since that morning, Sujata had stopped speaking. She went about her usual activities with a methodical rigor, but although she hugged the children as usual and played with them, she didn't say a word to anyone. It was like the gag was still in her mouth, Sachin thought, even after he'd removed it.

After the men had left, he had managed to wriggle across the floor to their bed, where he had found Sujata almost naked, her sari torn to shreds, and her choli hanging off one shoulder. He was able to position himself and untie her hands with his own still pinned behind his back while she lay as rigid as a corpse, weeping softly. After lying there for several minutes, she jumped up and ran into the bathroom, where he heard her retching. She dressed and went to check on the children who had not yet emerged from their room. Only then had she returned to untie him.

That night, Sachin slept on a blanket in the kitchen while Sujata lay, curled into a tight ball, on their bed. For three days, they lived like strangers, not saying a word to each other. Sachin kept the news from the neighbors, unable to face the questions and well-meaning offers of help that would inevitably arise. It was no use going to the police, for Govind Lala's influence far surpassed that of even Damodar. His largesse ensured the police would quickly forget about a case moments after Sachin filed a complaint.

Finally, Sujata broke her silence while she packed a small, wooden trunk that they had owned ever since they moved into the flat. She told him she was taking the children to her parents' house. She did not ask him when he would follow.

The flat seemed very large as Sachin wandered through it, trying to establish a new routine. Even the smallest task required extra effort as he relived the events of that fateful morning. Smoldering anger began to consume the few remaining shreds of his fear. He shuttered the shop an hour earlier than usual and walked across the courtyard to Major Kulkarni's flat. The major needed little convincing that Sachin wanted to protect his shop against future threats, and Sachin left with a handgun and several boxes of bullets.

The pavements still bustled with vendors hawking their wares, from clothes to small electrical appliances, as Sachin walked under the focused glow of the street lamps along Mount Road. He turned down a side street off Gunpowder Road and found himself in a narrow lane bordered by densely packed, crumbling houses that rose two and three stories high. Most of their faded, water-stained exteriors cried out for a fresh coat of paint. Battered wooden shutters hung open like outstretched hands, framing narrow window grilles. Ahead of Sachin, a small crowd gathered in front of a stone grotto in the middle of the lane. The grotto held a statue of a smiling woman in a blue robe. She appeared to be stepping on a snake. Sachin had visited Matharpacady just once before, but he knew the large Catholic population that inhabited the neighborhood had revered the grotto for many generations.

The people were chanting prayers in English that Sachin didn't entirely understand, but it sounded like they were repeating the same words over and over again. As he wove his way through the crowd, he saw that most of them fingered beads while they raised their heads to watch a makeshift screen—a bed sheet strung between bamboo poles above the grotto. A few feet away stood a man with a slide projector. Sachin stopped for a moment and raised his eyes to the screen. It depicted a man—he recognized him as the Christian god— being whipped. Sachin knew little of Christianity beyond the casual conversations he'd had with the Fernandes family, but he remembered that the broken, bent figure on the screen had eventually been killed. It seemed strange behavior for a god—to die powerless and defeated. He shook his head and continued through the mass of people. The droning voices rose and fell as he slipped past the grotto and into the empty lane behind it.

It had not been difficult to find out where Lobo lived. A few words to one of Sachin's regular customers, who had connections in Bombay's vast underground, had produced results within a day. It turned out that the informant belonged to a rival gang only too happy to share information that might result in Govind Lala's discomfiture. Sachin had expected to find Lobo in one of the posh Bandra or Santacruz neighborhoods, but his informant had assured him that the address in Matharpacady— less than a kilometer from his shop—was correct.

Sachin walked along a concrete wall that bordered the neighborhood, and the old stone houses and bungalows soon gave way to clusters of newer, high-rise buildings. He found one with the name St. Theresa Towers stenciled above the entrance. He debated whether to take the lift, then ended up walking up the narrow, dimly lit staircase to the third floor.

He rang the doorbell, breathing hard, his heart racing. He reached inside his pocket and closed his hand around the cold steel grip of the gun. Lobo answered the door. His bulging eyes grew even larger as he glared at Sachin.

"What the bleddy—"

"Shut up," Sachin hissed, shoving the gun through the gap in the door. Lobo's mouth opened, but he said nothing. He backed away from the door and Sachin followed, slamming it behind him.

He walked into a small living room that contained a pair of chairs set against one wall. Instead of a sofa, the opposite wall had a cot pushed up against it, on which a woman lay with her eyes closed. Wispy strands of ash-colored hair fell on either side of her sunken cheeks. A thin, checkered blanket covered her body. Her bony knees formed a small hill in the plateau of the fabric.

Lobo's eyes held a cold contempt that made Sachin pause. He pointed the gun at Lobo's head with one hand supporting the other, like he had seen in the movies.

"You must pay for what you did," Sachin said, not taking his eyes off Lobo's face. His voice sounded tinny and distant, as if he were listening to himself speaking on the radio.

Lobo looked at the gun, then back at Sachin's face. "You want to kill me, you bleddy bashturd? Go ahead, men. You'll be doing me a big favor."

Sachin blinked. "What…what do you mean?"

"Go ahead," Lobo repeated, nodding his head for emphasis. He spread his arms wide. "You see this? This is my bleddy life. I live here with my mother. She's dying, but it's a long, slow death. I take care of her. I make money doing Govind Lala's bleddy dirty work so I can pay her bleddy medical bills. Then I come home and wipe the bleddy shit from her bleddy ass." He folded his arms across his chest. "So go ahead, men, shoot me if you want. I don't give a fuck anymore."

Sachin took a step forward, his eyes narrowing as he stared at the vein pulsing in Lobo's forehead. Lobo's scowl remained frozen on his face. Sachin brought the gun closer and aimed it between Lobo's eyes, his finger cradling the trigger.

His chest heaved. He lowered his hand and backed up to the door. Lobo watched him in silence, standing motionless, arms still crossed.

The next morning, Sachin began his routine of opening the shop to prepare for another day. As the shutter rode halfway up the track, he paused. He wound it back down and climbed up the stairs to his empty flat.

Cats

SHE SHUFFLES ACROSS THE dusty marble floor, cats running through her. As Eleanor reaches the brass coffee table, she pauses and peers at the blurry outline of the grandfather clock. The fog that clouds her vision does not melt away, as much as she wills it, and the position of the clock's arms remains a mystery. With a sigh, she settles into her favorite overstuffed armchair, and three of the cats immediately assume their customary positions. They are the privileged ones, who have won the rights to Eleanor's chair not by prowess in battle but by virtue of seniority. Thomas, a dusky grey Burmese nestles between Eleanor's spare frame and the right arm of the chair, while Ginger, a female of unknown ancestry, occupies a similar spot on the left. Victoria, an Oriental shorthair with one functional and striking blue eye, perches on the back just beside Eleanor's head, observing the movements of the junior members of her clan with mild distaste that eventually yields to haughty indifference.

Eleanor reaches for the bell placed on the coffee table just within reach of her thin and mottled hand. She rings it with

the vigor of a woman considerably younger than her eighty-
six years. "Asha!" she cries, with surprising firmness. "Where
are you, girl?"

"Coming, memsahib." Her servant enters through an arched
doorway that leads to the kitchen. A damp dishrag is tucked
into the folds of her sari. She wipes her hands on it, fixing
Eleanor with an expectant stare.

"Asha, what time is it? Is the boy due today?"

"Half-past four, memsahib. He always comes on Wednesday.
He is probably just running late."

Neil Sequeira was indeed running late. A protracted after-
class discussion with his Hindi teacher ended with the usual
recommendation to engage a private tutor, or else Neil would
be in grave danger of failing his final exams. It so happened,
as a matter of the purest coincidence, that the Hindi teacher
also tutored several students after school and had a spot open
in his schedule. He dispatched Neil with a note to his parents,
informing them of their son's poor performance. It carried a
guarantee that the situation could be remedied by engaging his
services. The goal of passing the eighth-standard Hindi finals
was a certainty, the note said, with twice-weekly lessons for
only one hundred fifty rupees per week.

Now Neil races across the schoolyard and out the gate, free at
last. He stuffs the note into his tattered and faded backpack that
is on the verge of disgorging several textbooks. He slows down
as he approaches the familiar house, its yellow stucco exterior
a sharp contrast to the polished sandstone and reconstructed
brick of the school barely two hundred meters to its south. He
deposits his backpack on the porch beside the door.

Thomas and Ginger arrive at the door behind Asha, demanding their tribute, and Neil obliges by bowing low and scratching their chins. Satisfied with this declaration of fealty, the cats return to their places at Eleanor's side. Neil follows them while Asha returns to the kitchen to prepare tea.

"Hello, Aunty Eleanor. Sorry I'm late." Neil takes a seat across from Eleanor, after dislodging a stubborn but junior member of the clan. After a meow of protest, the unrepentant cat jumps back into Neil's lap and begins to purr.

"No matter, son. Was it the Hindi teacher again?"

Neil nods in agreement, and Eleanor tut-tuts in sympathy as she searches for something on the coffee table. "Ah, here it is. Tell me, Neil, what do you make of this letter? Asha's English doesn't stretch as far as reading, you see, and my eyes are too tired."

Neil unfolds the sheet of paper, noticing the revenue stamp at the bottom and the official seal of the Bombay Municipal Corporation. As he reads, a frown transforms his face. Although Neil is a voracious reader, with an appetite for rich and varied literary fare, the letter before him does not require much intellectual exertion to divine its meaning. Written in the terse, unimaginative prose of the civil servant, it is punctuated by the occasional malapropism, betraying the writer's native language as one other than English. Neil hands the letter back to Eleanor. His frown deepens.

"Well, what does it say?"

Neil hesitates. "They can't do this. I'm sure they can't!"

"Do what, dear boy?"

Neil falls silent again. As Thomas decides to vacate his position of power on Eleanor's chair in favor of one at Neil's feet, Neil begins his account. "The BMC is seizing your house, under the Citizen's Land Owner Act of Maharashtra. The act was passed last month. It requires all property held by former British officers to be repossessed by the state, unless the owner is currently an Indian citizen."

Eleanor sits upright, with glassy eyes that appear fixed on the far wall. Only the trembling of her left hand as she strokes Ginger's neck hints at any emotion.

Neil continues, "You have to evacuate the house by December 1...less than three months away. Aunty Eleanor, this can't happen. I won't let it!"

A hint of a smile breaks Eleanor's vacant expression. "Dear boy, there's not much we can do, it seems." Her level tone jars Neil's senses much more than the outburst he expected.

Neil squirms in his chair, fiddling with his rosary beads while trying to avoid his mother's glare. The Sequeiras follow the practice, as do many Goan families, of praying the rosary every day. Much to the annoyance of the Sequeira children, however, their parents have decreed that the ritual must be completed before dinner is served. As a result, the children do their best to speed up the process. As Neil appears to listen to his older brother leading the first decade, his mind wrestles with more weighty matters.

Hail Mary, full of grace...could she rent a place in Byculla, in that colony where the old people live?

The Lord is with thee...but what would happen to the cats? They don't allow animals there. No, that wouldn't work.

Blessed art thou amongst women...maybe she could move in with Aunty June, who'd definitely be glad to have the company? She does have a lot of room in her flat, with two extra bedrooms. He'll have to talk to her about it. Maybe he could call her tonight.

"Neil!" grunts his father. "Your turn."

With a start, Neil realizes that it's already time for the second decade, which he leads. He looks at his sister, Anne, who appears to be lost in a warm, comforting place, far removed from rosaries. "You take it," he says. He tosses the beads onto his chair and runs into his bedroom.

After the litanies have been recited and the closing prayers concluded, Sheila finds her son face down on his bed, clutching the pillow with both hands. "What's wrong, Neil?" she says, placing a hand on his shoulder. Neil offers no answer, his body as stiff as the unornamented teak headboard. Then, suddenly, he exhales and his body goes limp. He offers a disjointed recounting of Eleanor's predicament.

Sheila listens without interrupting, but her broad forehead creases. "Why don't we talk to your cousin Nancy? She works for that law firm in Girgaum. I'm sure she knows someone who can help. I'll call her tomorrow morning."

Neil rolls over and swings his feet off the bed. "Thanks, mom."

When Neil returns from school the next day, his mother informs him that Nancy has promised to talk to one of the lawyers at her office, who has a lot of experience working with the BMC. He sounds like the perfect candidate for the job. Neil's eyes brighten at the prospect, but Sheila warns him not to get his hopes up too soon. "We don't know if he can do anything yet," she says. She opens a pack of Parle Gluco biscuits and places them on the table in front of Neil. "And besides, he may be very expensive. I'm not sure if Eleanor will be able to afford him."

Neil nods, his enthusiasm undampened by these cautionary words. Like the final chapters in all the Enid Blyton books he read at an early age, he feels that all will end well.

Later that week, he returns to Eleanor's house after school. Asha lets him in with a look of surprise, telling him that it's not Wednesday. Unfazed by the chronological disruption, Thomas and Ginger detach themselves from the group by the armchair and begin to rub against Neil's ankles. They purr with contentment as he bows to tickle their chins. Soon, they tire of the attention and walk away, their tails held high.

Eleanor receives the news without comment, merely nodding. Neil gets the sense that she is far away that evening, as their conversation trickles out like the last remnants of water in a faucet during one of the frequent outages. Neil watches, unsure how to cut through the dense silence, as Eleanor gathers two more of the cats into her lap. Thomas mews with displeasure at this unexpected turn of events, but she doesn't seem to notice him either.

Asha intervenes and asks Neil if he would like some tea and biscuits. He thanks her but declines, saying he needs to get home. He stops at the door. "Don't worry, Aunty Eleanor," he says, as he hoists his backpack onto one shoulder. "Everything will be all right. You'll see."

Eleanor waves the ghost of a hand in his direction but says nothing.

When Neil returns home, the sound of the stereo fills the flat. Anne has cranked the volume up in the living room so she can hear it in the kitchen. Neil recognizes one of her favorites,

As Tears Go By. Not by the Stones, but the second version by Marianne Faithfull after her voice deepened an octave. Their parents are out at a church meeting, Anne says. She's in charge of cooking, so she gets to play the stereo as loud as she wants.

Neil helps in the kitchen, peeling potatoes and cleaning rice. He wonders if dinner will be late enough that they'll miss the rosary. He asks Anne if their mother has heard anything more from the law office, but Anne is oblivious, singing along to Faithfull's whiskey-tinged, smoky vocals as she stirs assorted vegetables into a stainless steel pot. After two more join it, bubbling on the stove, Neil tells Anne about Eleanor. She continues singing but offers no suggestions.

In his bedroom, Neil watches the solitary black Molly swim around an aquarium filled with iridescent guppies. The tank catches the fading sunlight that streams through the open window.

He started the aquarium a few months before he first met Eleanor. In the third standard, although he saw the cottage every day on his way to and from school, Neil never gave it a second thought. That day, as he passed the stone archway that framed the entrance to the compound, he heard a soft meowing. He hesitated, debating whether to ignore it and move on. After a moment he heard it again, more insistent this time. His mind made up, he walked through the archway, scanning the unkempt row of shrubs that lined a narrow path.

He soon discovered a small black and white cat under the bushes. One of its feet was caught in a dense tangle of vines at the base of a night jasmine shrub. The cat looked up at him, pleading with its big green eyes. He bent down to try and calm it by stroking its chin. It rubbed its head against him, and he scratched it behind one ear as his other hand crept toward the trapped paw. He feared that the cat would lash out at him if he moved too fast, but it showed no sign of aggression. Soon he had freed the paw and scooped the cat into his arms. It uttered only a mild protest.

He walked along the path until he came to the front of the house. An untidy clump of rose bushes grew on either side of a portico that framed the entrance. The faded stucco had crumbled in places, leaving gaping scars on the yellow surface, and the door was missing a hinge. He climbed the rough-cut stone steps that led to the front porch, the cat still tucked under one arm, and looked for a doorbell. There appeared to be none, but he spied a thick rope that emerged from one side of the doorframe, wrapped around a rusted iron pulley. The free end of the rope had a thick knot that hung at eye level. He pulled the rope. A cavernous clanging resounded inside the house.

Almost afraid to discover what lay within the decrepit building, he considered simply taking the cat home with him. It nuzzled his chest, its body warm against his bare arms. As Neil was about to turn away, the door opened, and a woman peered out. Her hair gleamed as white as a mogra flower garland. An intricate network of wrinkles crisscrossed her face, from which watery blue eyes—a shade he'd never seen before—regarded him with a hint of suspicion. Then she spotted his burden, and they flooded with relief.

"Oh, thank goodness!" she said, in a reedy but loud voice that made Neil jump. "You've found Sir Lancelot. I noticed he was missing an hour ago, but my servant has already left, you see, and I haven't been able to search for him. Come in, come in, dear boy!"

Neil wasn't entirely sure he should follow. He was about to make some excuse to leave, but a sidelong glance past the old woman heightened his sense of curiosity. He walked into a dimly lit parlor and placed the squirming bundle on the tiled floor. Sir Lancelot meowed with what Neil assumed was pleasure and bounded away. As Neil's eyes adjusted to the tomb-like darkness—he realized that heavy drapes were drawn across all the windows—he noticed several cats scattered around the sparsely furnished room. Two were draped on the arms of a worn but spacious high-backed armchair, and three others lounged at strategic points on a sofa that sported the same pea-green and gold upholstery as the chair.

The woman introduced herself as Eleanor Lewis. While the cats wandered about—it seemed like more and more of them were emerging from distant corners of the house—she poured out her story. She told Neil how she'd come to India when her husband was assigned to the Bombay shipyards in the 1930s. He was one of the few servicemen who decided to remain behind after India's independence, and he spent a large part of his time training officers in the Indian navy. The old cottage was a retirement gift, but he'd died a few years after they moved in. Although they had no children, Eleanor continued to live in the large, empty house with only her cats and a succession of part-time servants for company.

Soon, Neil found himself returning to the cottage on a regular basis. Eleanor expected him every Wednesday and regaled him with stories from her past while Asha served biscuits and steaming hot tea. Eleanor showed Neil several photo albums with dog-eared, charcoal pages that held yellowing pictures of her husband and their friends. He reciprocated with his first pictures of the new aquarium.

Neil sighs now, as he watches the fish continue their endless circumnavigation of the tank. He tries to pin down a logical reason for the turmoil Eleanor's impending eviction has stirred in him. Finding none, he heads off to the kitchen in search of dinner.

Several days elapse before Sheila finds herself in the lawyer's office, on the sixth floor of a newer high-rise building near Saifee Hospital in Girgaum. He hears her story with impassive attention, then agrees to an initial consultation with Eleanor at no charge. At first, he shakes his head when Sheila explains the meeting will have to be at Eleanor's house, but he resigns himself to the unorthodox arrangement. "Just for Nancy's sake, you understand." He begins to gush about how much he admires Nancy's work. Sheila suspects his effusive praise isn't merely from professional interest but says nothing, deciding it's none of her business anyway.

Neil receives the news with barely contained excitement, even though Sheila cautions that it's too early to start celebrating just yet. He floats through the next few days like a feather carried by the wind until Wednesday arrives.

Asha answers the door, her sari coming loose at the waist and her hair disheveled. She looks as if she has been working all night. "Memsahib is not feeling well," she says. "She has been in bed since yesterday. She sends her regrets, very sorry, but she is not seeing anyone. I am staying here only, full time now."

Neil's heart sinks, and the anticipation that lifted his spirits evaporates in an instant, leaving a dull, featureless ache. He promises to return that weekend and hopes Eleanor will be better by then. Asha nods. She tells him that his visit would probably do more good than the doctor who came early that morning. "That old goat fussed and prodded memsahib for half an hour," Asha says, shaking her head. "Memsahib complained he was interrupting her sleep. She told him to get out."

At the end of the school week, Neil escapes the clutches of the Hindi teacher by announcing he'll be signing up for private tutoring at last. Once again, Asha opens the door in response to his summons. His heart sinks as she struggles to greet him. Her eyes are hollow and dark stains streak her cheeks. Without bothering to switch to her broken English, she tells him that Eleanor died the previous night.

Neil reaches for the doorpost to steady himself. A strange emptiness begins to tear away at him from inside, consuming his body piece by piece. As Asha's tears flow, unhindered, his own eyes begin to sting. Asha places a shaking hand on his shoulder. They stand in the doorway together. A few of the cats come over to investigate.

It is not the first funeral that Neil has attended, but it seems more real to him than the others. A year earlier, his aunt Ellie died, and he joined his family on crowded charter buses to the Sewri cemetery, following Mass at St. Magnus Church. After a brief service at the gravesite, he waited in line for his chance to toss a spoonful of dirt into the grave.

This time, only a few people occupy the front pews of the church. Neil wears an ill-fitting, stiff-collared shirt and gray tie. He squirms on the unyielding wood of the pew. At regular intervals, he casts a longing glance at his watch. There are no buses afterwards, so his father hails a taxi. A light drizzle prompts his parents to unfurl umbrellas, but Neil lets the misty droplets soak his hair, making it curl more than usual. As he stands with his head bowed, his mother inquires about the gravesite location.

At length, the priest and undertakers arrive, and a few people from the church assemble around the damp piles of earth that surround the pit. A system of squeaky pulleys and strips of woven jute lowers the coffin. As he watches the polished mahogany box sink lower, Neil wonders if Asha will remember to feed the cats that night.

A week later, Sheila receives a phone call from the lawyer at Nancy's office. He asks whether they can meet. When Sheila presses him, he reveals that it concerns Neil as well. Accordingly, they decide on an appointment after Neil is done with school that day, and he makes the concession of promising to stop by their flat.

The lawyer is already seated in a Rexine-clad chairs when Neil arrives home. Without preamble, he tells Neil that Eleanor has deeded the house to him in her will. It will be held in the name of a trust until Neil turns twenty-one, at which time he will receive full title to the property.

Neil squeezes his eyes shut. Long moments pass, then he opens them and glances at Sheila for help. She clings to him, expressing her joy at the news. But Neil's chest tightens as an amorphous darkness reaches for him, dragging him deeper into the earth along with Eleanor's mortal remains.

After the lawyer leaves, Neil tells Sheila that he must break the news to Asha. When Asha lets him in, he hesitates, buying time by entertaining the cats. After running out of small talk, he describes the arrangement. She reacts with disbelief at first, but then peppers him with questions about her own fate, to which he has no answers at the moment. Muttering to herself, Asha retires to the kitchen. Neil perches on the edge of the old sofa and closes his eyes.

A warm, furry body rubs against his ankles. He opens his eyes, scoops Sir Lancelot into his arms, and walks to the bank of windows across from the sofa. Still cradling the cat with one arm, he pulls the cords with a snap, opening the drapes at each window in turn. The orange glow of the setting sun floods the parlor. One by one, the cats gather at Neil's feet, bathed in soft light.

The Wedding Gift

INCENT LOOKED AROUND THE ROOM, wrinkling his nose as he tried to locate the source of the smell. It permeated everything, clinging to clothes, bedsheets, and the fabric of the furniture. It even saturated his hair, like rotting cabbage. Except he knew it wasn't rotting cabbage. It was the latest reminder of his instinctive reluctance when he'd first heard of the scheme concocted by their parents.

They had moved into the flat the day before, giddy with anticipation at the prospect of having their own place in a good Bandra neighborhood off Linking Road. Vincent knew flats in this part of Bombay were impossible to find and well beyond the means of a newly married couple.

"It's not a loan," his father insisted. "Mr. Gomes and I talked it over, and we agreed to split the cost. He has plenty of cash available from the time he worked in the Gulf, and your mother and I certainly don't need such a big place now that all you kids are gone. We'll sell our flat, move someplace smaller. We'll be fine."

At first, Vincent protested his parents' decision, especially when he discovered their new flat was in Vasai, over an hour away. In spite of his father's reassurances, Vincent knew they didn't have the kind of money that Diana's family took for granted. Arguing with his parents didn't help, for they shrugged off all his objections. They wanted to do this, they said, for their youngest son—the only one still living in Bombay—and their minds were made up.

Diana, on the other hand, offered only a token resistance. Perhaps it had something to do with being an only child. Vincent would never understand how that felt, having grown up with four siblings. In the end, when they signed the contract, both of them had realized how much they'd wanted a home to call their own. Even if the building was named Pearly Gates.

Vincent walked around the bedroom, shaking his head. He stepped over boxes yet to be unpacked. "I don't think it's in here," Diana said, after he'd completed a circuit along the freshly painted walls. "The smell of the paint hides it a little, but..."

He nodded. They'd noticed a hint of the strange odor the day before but had been too busy wrestling with boxes and rearranging furniture to give it much thought. Probably just a clogged drain, Vincent had said.

Diana eased herself off the bed and reached behind to tie her hair into a ponytail. Vincent watched her as she stretched, still unable to believe it wasn't all a dream. The six weeks they'd spent in a room at his parents' old flat, as spacious as it was, had been awkward at best. The initial thrill of exploring each other's bodies had been quickly offset by the need to keep noise levels down, something Diana found especially difficult. It was one of the little things he loved about her.

She caught him staring at her and smiled, her eyes beckoning. "Think how much we can enjoy our first night here," she whispered, "if we can get rid of this fucking smell. It's a good thing we didn't sleep here last night."

Although he'd known Diana for over two years, Vincent still hadn't got used to her swearing. She'd never been the slightest bit apologetic. The only time she made a conscious effort to behave like a lady, she said, was with his parents. Especially his mother, whose life revolved around rosaries, novenas, and daily Mass.

Vincent sighed and walked out of the bedroom, still sniffing. Diana followed close behind, a teasing hand caressing the small of his back. As they entered the kitchen, he groaned and clapped a hand over his nose. "Oh God," he said, "it's awful."

He prowled around the kitchen like a lion circling its prey. As he approached the sink, he uncovered his nose and bent over the drain. Immediately, he jumped back and Diana giggled. "Run some water down it," she said.

He opened the faucet and water gurgled into the sink. With his hand back in place over his nose, he waited for a few seconds before turning the water off. If anything, the stench had intensified.

He crouched low and opened the door under the sink. At once, he staggered back, hitting his head against the cabinets that lined the opposite wall. "It's in here," he said, gasping for breath. He surveyed the open floor drain under the pipe that carried wastewater from the sink. "Get me a torch."

A quick sweep with the beam revealed that the saucer-shaped cover lay beside the floor drain, instead of over it. Vincent stood upright and picked up a kitchen towel from the counter. He tied it around his mouth and nose, provoking a fresh bout of giggles from Diana. "You look ridiculous," she said.

Vincent got down on his knees and adjusted his improvised mask. Armed with the torch, he stuck his head into the narrow space under the sink, bending his shoulders back.

His mask didn't appear to be helping, as the odor assaulted his nostrils, and the room began spinning around him. With a determined movement, he aimed the light down the exposed drain, peering into what little part of it he could see. Then, as realization dawned on him, he scooted backwards, dropping the torch with a metallic clang on the cold, hard tiles.

"Something's in there," he said, clutching at the bright yellow Formica countertop to steady himself. "Something dead."

Diana's eyes opened wide, and her giggles evaporated, replaced by a look of pure horror.

Vincent's eyes scanned the kitchen counter. "The tongs," he said, pointing to a drawer at the far end of the row. "Give me the tongs."

With the cast iron tongs in one hand, Vincent prepared himself for the next maneuver. He moved the trash can until it was sitting just beside the open cabinet door, then dived under the sink again. After feeling around with the tongs, he clamped them tight and began to pull upward, being careful not to dislodge their cargo. A fuzzy, gray blob emerged into the light. He backed out, trying not to bump his head on the cabinet frame, and threw the tongs into the trash.

With the mask still obscuring his face, Vincent tied the bag and ran down three flights of stairs to the courtyard, where garbage containers were stacked against one wall. He tossed the bag into the nearest one.

"What was it?" Diana asked, as he washed his hands with copious amounts of dish soap.

He shrugged. "Looked like a rat."

By the next morning, the smell had dissipated, helped along its way by the incense sticks Diana insisted on burning in every room. She'd been too spooked by the incident to do much more than toss and turn in bed most of the night. Vincent had decided, with more than a little regret, that their night of celebration would have to wait.

That evening, he came home from work with a bottle of wine and—at Diana's request, for she didn't feel like cooking—Chinese food from a restaurant down the road.

She had set up the stereo in the living room, and strains of an Air Supply song wafted into the kitchen as he rummaged through the newly stocked shelves for some plates. He wasn't a big Air Supply fan, but he knew this album was one of her favorites.

After dinner, they cleared the table and left the dishes soaking in the sink. By mutual consent, they decided not to check the drain again. As the music swelled, Diana led him into the living room where they settled into the comforting embrace of an overstuffed sofa. Their wine glasses waited on a small, hand-carved mahogany end table. They'd bought it a week earlier at Khadi Emporium, Diana's favorite place to browse for knick-knacks, and where she invariably ended up spending too much.

Her smile lit up her face, reminding Vincent of how she'd looked when he'd asked her to marry him. As they clinked glasses for the second time that evening, Vincent wondered again if it was all a dream, whether he'd wake up in his parents' flat, in the bedroom he'd occupied as long as he could remember. He put down his glass and took Diana's hand, drawing her close. The subtle scent of sandalwood soap blended with the honey-sweet overtones of parijata attar, making his head spin. He kissed the long, slender curve of her neck as she ran her fingers through his hair.

He stood up and gathered her in his arms, their bodies melding together. As he drowned in the sensation of her moist, warm lips on his, the doorbell rang.

She twisted away, tidying her hair, and frowned. "Let's ignore it," Vincent said, lowering his voice. He tried to lead her toward the bedroom, but she shook her head.

A pair of wrinkled faces framed by long, gray hair peered around the door as Diana opened it.

"I hope we're not interrupting your dinner," one of them said. "We came by last night, but you must have been out. We just wanted to welcome you to the building."

Diana invited the two women in, assuring them they weren't interrupting at all. Vincent forced a smile as he greeted them. They introduced themselves as Apama and Manjula Shah from A12, and handed him a heavy bowl of aromatic vegetable biryani, still warm. "A little gift, please. To celebrate your new home," Apama said as they sat down on the sofa.

They'd been among the first residents in the A block of Pearly Gates, Manjula said, almost thirty years ago. Since they were the only two women in their family who never married, they'd decided to buy a flat together. From then on, they made it a point to greet new residents when they moved in. "Just ask us only," Apama said, "if you need anything. After all, we are both being retired now. So much time we have."

Over the next hour, Vincent and Diana listened to stories about almost everyone in A block. Apparently, some of them were more worthy of attention than others. Mr. Gilani, a young man on the second floor, worked at a call center and slept most of the day. Another couple, Mr. and Mrs. Shetty, occupied the flat across the hall from Vincent and Diana. They had two teenage daughters whom they allowed out at all odd hours of the night. And, of course, there was Miss Khalili on the ground floor, in A2—almost thirty and still unmarried, Manjula whispered. The sisters never knew quite what she did, as she wasn't in the habit of socializing with other residents. But they'd observed a constant stream of men coming and going in the time she'd lived there. "I don't like to think this thing or that," Manjula said, arching her eyebrows, "but you only decide. That woman, something is not right."

After repeating their offer to help if Vincent and Diana needed anything, the two women left. Vincent watched Diana's face as she struggled to control herself, then they both burst out laughing. "Every building has its resident gossips," he said, wiping a hand across his eyes. "Still, that biryani smells really good."

Diana snuggled against him and looked into his eyes. She brushed a stray curl away from his forehead and trailed her fingertips down to his lips. "I believe you had something else in mind, Mr. D'Costa."

They tripped over boxes and unruly piles of clothing in their haste to reach the bedroom. As Vincent fumbled with Diana's clothes, he noticed the open window. For a moment, he wondered whether he should shut it, but the thought evaporated as Diana pulled him under the thin cotton bedcover. They made love like it was the first time, with a hunger that Vincent had missed during their awkward, constrained sessions at his parents' flat. Diana's low, languorous moans grew in intensity as she writhed beneath him. Her nails dug into his back. In response, he slid his hands around her hips and began to thrust faster, until she cried out with an abandon that pushed him over the edge as well.

As they lay in their new bed on sweat-soaked sheets, Vincent said, "I wonder if those two old ladies have good hearing." He flinched as Diana smacked his chest.

Vincent picked up the handset of the black, boxy telephone that sat on a sideboard in the living room. No dial tone greeted him, and he slammed it back into its cradle. They'd paid the customary bribe just to get the connection set up and avoid the normal months-long wait. The telephone serviceman had arrived the day before with the phone but said he had to confirm the service at the Bandra exchange. He'd promised it would only be a day or two.

"Diana? The phone still isn't working. I'm going downstairs to the paan shop to make a call, okay?"

Diana emerged from the bathroom wrapped in a towel, her glistening hair leaving rivulets of water trailing down her back. "Don't be too long. My parents will be here in less than an hour."

Vincent ran down the stairs, not bothering to wait for the notoriously slow lift. When he arrived at the ground-floor landing, he saw a man waiting outside A2. Vincent mumbled a greeting, but the man avoided his eyes. The door opened, and Vincent stopped, drawn against his will to the liquid brown eyes that stared back at him. He took a long, slow breath, savoring the woman's hair, tinted with henna, that cascaded to her slender shoulders. His throat went dry as he gazed at her delicate nose that led to full, cherry-red lips. They parted slightly, as if whispering a welcome.

The door shut behind the man, breaking the trance. In the few days that Vincent and Diana had lived at Pearly Gates, they'd heard more stories about Miss Khalili from the other neighbors, all in general agreement with the opinion expressed by the Shah sisters. Until now, Vincent had only caught the briefest glimpse of the woman one morning as he left for work. He shook his head, trying to wash away the image of her face.

The next morning, the phone was still dead. Diana promised to call him at work if the exchange fixed the problem. She had to make a few calls herself now that she'd decided to start looking for a job. The dinner with her parents had turned sour as soon as she'd told them. Why did their daughter need to work, they said, when they could provide all the money she needed? Vincent wasn't sure how Diana would handle her first full-time job, but he knew she didn't want to spend all day at home. Besides, they both hated the idea of being even further indebted to her parents. She'd argued with them late into the night, ending it only by storming off into the bedroom and locking the door. Her parents had given up and gone home, finally realizing there was little they could do to stop her.

That stubborn streak had fascinated him ever since they'd met. He was at the library, poring over class notes for his third-year prelim exams, when he overheard an animated discussion that rose above the background chatter. Looking up, he saw a girl at the next table gesticulating wildly, eyes flashing as she drove home her point to her companion. They appeared to be discussing the finer points of Dickens' *The Old Curiosity Shop.*

"How can you read that stuff?" her friend said as Vincent stared, fascinated in spite of himself by the passion in those liquid brown eyes. "He's so boring, yaar. Honestly, if we weren't studying the novel, I would never read anything by him."

The girl raised her eyebrows and thumped a fist on the table. "He is not boring! He happens to be the greatest Victorian novelist of all time, and—what are you staring at?"

Vincent's pulse pounded in his ears. "Sorry," he said, unable to tear his eyes away from her face. "I couldn't help overhearing, and it's just that...well...I've read almost all his books."

She flung a triumphant look at the other girl. "Well, then," she said, "you can convince my friend that she doesn't know what the fuck she's talking about, can't you?"

After that first encounter, they discovered more shared interests besides literature. Even when they didn't agree—especially when it came to music, he preferring classic rock and she pop—it seemed to strengthen the bond between them. After Vincent graduated, they continued to see each other regularly. The following year, he asked Diana to marry him.

Her parents opposed the marriage at first, but they'd learned, from years of experience, that their only daughter usually got her way. Soon, the two families became inseparable, and Vincent's parents accepted Diana as their own child long before the actual wedding. In fact, Vincent had realized, it often seemed like Diana had a better relationship with his parents than she did with her own.

Vincent stared at the telephone now, willing it to come to life. It took almost a week before he was able to make his first call to his parents. "We have a normal flat now," he said, "with telephone service like everyone else."

"Any luck with the job search?" he asked Diana, as they cuddled on the couch, paying little attention to the television.

She shrugged. "I haven't seen too many opportunities for someone with a BA in English. Besides, I didn't want to apply for anything before the phone was fixed."

"If you want, I can ask a few people at work." He stroked her hair as she leaned against him. "Just last week, someone was talking about this company, Solindia. Their office is near Opera House. They make solar panels or something, and they're always hiring sales people. All they want is a college degree."

Diana's lips quivered. "Honestly, do you think I can sell solar panels?"

Vincent shrugged. "It may be worth finding out. In fact, I think this guy I used to know from St. Boniface works there— Peter Braganza. I could give him a call, see what he says. At least until something else—"

A loud crash interrupted them, followed by the sound of raised voices from across the hallway. Diana jumped up and peered out the peephole.

"What is it?" Vincent said, not particularly inclined to get up from the sofa. Diana held up a hand.

"They must be fighting again," she whispered. "I just saw one of the girls come running out."

"They fight a lot." He stood up and yawned. "Maybe that's what we'll be like when we have kids."

She stepped away from the door and glared at him, hands on her hips. "I hope not. I hope we're never that bad. Do you think we should do something?"

"Do what?"

She came back to the sofa, wringing her hands. "I don't know. I just feel like we should help."

Vincent sighed. "Best not to get involved."

A few nights later when Vincent returned from work, a scribbled note greeted him at the entrance to A block: "Lift is broken." He swore under his breath and began trudging up the stairs when Miss Khalili emerged from A2. Vincent gazed at the vision, transfixed by the pale yellow salwar kameez that clung to her body as if it had been painted on. The low-cut neck offered him a tantalizing glimpse of her cleavage, an expanse of smooth, flawless skin several shades lighter than his own. His eyes traveled lower, to her narrow waist and the gentle curve of her hips. Once again, he found himself caught in a spell that she seemed to cast without even knowing it.

Her lips curled as he raised his eyes. "Like what you see?"

He almost dropped his briefcase. His cheeks blazed. "What? No...I mean—"

Her glossy lips parted to reveal white, even teeth. She laughed, tossing her hair back. "It's okay. I'm used to it. You're Vincent D'Costa, right?"

He nodded, suddenly speechless.

"My name is Muneera. Nice to meet you." With that, she turned and walked down the hallway, leaving a lingering trace of rose attar—a more subtle scent than the ones Diana favored.

Vincent arrived at their flat, panting, just as Diana opened the door. She grabbed the front of his shirt and pulled him inside for a prolonged kiss.

"Welcome home," she breathed in his ear, when she finally disengaged.

He smiled. "What's the occasion?"

She pouted, then fluttered her eyelashes. "What do you mean? Can't I give my husband a proper greeting if I feel like it?"

He grinned and kissed her again, tasting a hint of cinnamon on her lips.

"Come on," he said, as she danced away from him. "Tell me what's going on. You're practically floating."

"I have a job interview tomorrow. It's at a private school here in Bandra—St. Theresa's—as a teacher's assistant."

A strange mixture of emotions bubbled up inside him, but he managed a smile. "That's great! I hope you get the job. If you don't, I'll have to call them and tell them they're making a huge mistake."

She bounced past him into the kitchen.

"Don't you dare," she said, raising her voice over the sound of running water.

The next time Vincent saw Muneera, he was standing at the bus stop just down the road from the building. She caught him by surprise, calling out his name.

"Where are you going? I'm taking a cab—can I offer you a lift?"

"My office is in Goregaon," he said, "near the Parsi temple, but please don't go to any trouble. I take the bus every day."

She smiled. As he squinted through his sunglasses, he noticed she wasn't wearing any makeup. "I'm going shopping in Malad. You're right on the way. Come on, it will save you some time."

He hesitated for a moment before thanking her. Several taxis waited just beyond the bus stop, and she picked the closest one.

"So, Vincent," she said, as the driver pulled into the morning traffic, honking his horn, "what do you do?"

"I'm a laboratory technician," he said, "at Anderson Chemical. Basically, I do all the dirty work the other chemists don't want to do. Washing glassware, preparing solutions, calibrating the instruments, and such." Then, before he could catch himself: "How about you?"

She threw her head back and laughed, a delicate, musical sound unlike Diana's full-throated chuckles. "Why, haven't you heard? I'm a prostitute."

He opened his mouth but shut it again without a word. Her eyes glittered like the tiny sequins that ringed the neck of her kameez—with considerable relief, he noted it was cut much higher this time. He still couldn't tell if she was pulling his leg.

As if reading his thoughts, she continued. "I came to Bombay a year ago from a small town in Gujarat, near Ahmedabad, after my father died. I thought I could make it here because I had a cousin who worked in the fashion industry. He promised his friend could find me a modeling job." She frowned, and the glow in her eyes faded. "The only problem was I had to take off all my clothes to get it."

Vincent shifted in the warm Rexine seat. "I'm sorry...look, you don't have to tell me this if it makes you uncomfortable."

Their eyes met, and some of the fire returned to hers. "Does it make *you* uncomfortable?"

He looked away as the taxi swerved to avoid a handcart that appeared out of nowhere. "A little, I guess. After all, I've never really talked to a prostitute before."

She laughed again. "At least you're honest."

After his initial discomfort wore off, Vincent found himself listening with fascination as Muneera told him how she was almost thrown out into the street because she couldn't pay the rent at her first flat. That was when one of her model friends told her about a call-girl agency that operated in Bandra. The money was good, her friend said, and the clients were always prescreened to minimize any trouble.

At first, she promised herself she'd only do it until she could find a real job. Soon she was making more money than she could ever hope for in the highly competitive modeling industry—or most others, for that matter.

Without understanding exactly how it happened, Vincent realized they were conversing like old friends. In turn, he began telling Muneera about how he met Diana and even about the darker days when he'd almost dropped out of college.

Before he knew it, the taxi was pulling over in front of the main entrance to Anderson Chemical. He thanked Muneera as he got out.

"Thank you for listening," she said. "You know, you're the only person in our building who doesn't turn his nose up at me. Even the men do it, after they're done mentally undressing me."

He thought about his own reaction the first time they'd met and hung his head.

That weekend, Diana's parents stopped by with grand plans for decorating the flat. Vincent let them indulge their fantasies, but he had little intention of following through. It was something neither he nor Diana cared that much about—it didn't really matter if the walls were gray instead of titian or if the bathroom floor was standard concrete instead of ceramic tiles.

Most of the time, Vincent didn't mind the company of Diana's parents, but he barely responded to their questions as they bustled around the flat, armed with notepads, textile swatches, and catalogs. At an opportune moment, he mumbled an excuse and left the flat to make a trip to the general store.

When he returned, Diana burst into the living room, stomping her feet.

"Can you believe it!" she yelled. "My dad doesn't want me to take that job. If I get it, that is."

Vincent dropped the bags he was holding on the floor. "Why not?"

She shrugged, then waved her hands. "Oh, you know mom and dad. Their precious daughter is too good for this kind of common labor."

A smirk formed on Vincent's face, but he wiped it off as he came under the full force of her glare. "So when do you hear back from the school?"

"They promised to make a decision by the end of next week. And to hell with what mom and dad think. If I get this job, I'm taking it. If not this one, then the next. I'm not going to put up with their shit anymore." She stomped out of the room, her gold bangles jingling like wind chimes in a gale.

Sighing, Vincent picked up the bags and took them into the kitchen. He knew Diana wouldn't let this go, and she wouldn't be satisfied until she had found a job. He wondered how his own parents felt about Diana working. His mother had broached the subject of children well before the wedding, and he suspected Diana's mother had done the same with her. He and Diana had discussed it briefly, but they'd agreed to wait for a few years—something unheard of in their parents' generation.

That night at dinner, Vincent urged Diana not to let her parents get to her. "Just because they paid for this flat," he said, shoveling a load of sorpotel and rice into his mouth, "doesn't mean they own us."

She nodded. "I know. It's just that sometimes they make me feel like a little girl again. It drives me fucking crazy." She reached across the table for the bowl of raita that she'd prepared the night before. As she lifted her spoon, a door slammed, and they heard Mrs. Shetty wailing—a high-pitched, keening sound.

They looked at each other, unsure what to do. Mr. Shetty's voice cut through the noise, and although he spoke in his perfect, precise Delhi Hindi, they could understand every word. Heavy footsteps thumped down the stairs.

Diana stood up. "I can't stand this," she said. "I'm going to see if she's okay." Vincent waited until he'd finished chewing, wiping the corner of his mouth with a starched linen napkin. With a lingering reluctance, he followed her into the hallway.

Diana rang the doorbell. "Mrs. Shetty? It's Diana. Are you okay?"

After a long moment, the door opened. Tears ran down Mrs. Shetty's plump cheeks, streaking her thick layer of makeup.

"I don't mean to interfere," Diana said, twisting her dupatta around one finger, "but is there anything I can do to help?"

Mrs. Shetty dabbed at her eyes with the end of her sari. "Please, come in," she said, her voice shaking. She showed them into a living room furnished much like their own, except considerably untidier, with magazines and books strewn everywhere. Diana sat next to Mrs. Shetty on a large leather sofa while Vincent paced the room across from them until he noticed Diana's frown. He settled into a matching armchair and studied his fingernails.

"I don't know what to say," Mrs. Shetty said in Hindi. She continued to wipe her eyes. "The bastard has left me."

Diana clucked her tongue and took Mrs. Shetty's hand. "I suppose I should not have confronted him about it," Mrs. Shetty continued, "but after months of lying, he finally admitted it. He has been seeing that...that whore. The Khalili woman."

Vincent's head shot up, and a strange, strangled sound escaped his throat. Diana's eyes were fixed on Mrs. Shetty, and she paid him no attention.

"I'm so sorry," Diana said. She stole a glance at the bedroom door. "Are the girls—"

Mrs. Shetty shook her head. "They're out with their friends. They don't know yet."

Vincent sat frozen in place while Diana interjected with sympathetic noises and polite agreement as Mrs. Shetty's tale unfolded. They'd been having difficulties for over a year, she said. Although she suspected her husband was cheating on her, she hadn't said a word to him about it. Then he began disappearing at night—taking a walk, he said, so he could sleep better. One of the servants in the building told her she'd seen Mr. Shetty going into A2. The next night, Mrs. Shetty had tiptoed downstairs after her husband left for his walk to see it happen with her own eyes.

They left after Diana promised to stop by the next day, to help with the housework and cook a meal for Mrs. Shetty, who protested that she was quite capable of doing these things herself. Vincent said nothing but let Diana continue her tirade as she disparaged Mr. Shetty's character and called for vengeance to be exacted on him in a number of lurid and painstakingly descriptive ways. At length, she paused to catch her breath.

"You're very quiet." She took a sip of water from a glass on the nightstand. As she began undressing, Vincent told her about his conversation with Muneera.

Vincent left early the next morning. He stopped as he got to the ground floor, tucked his briefcase under one arm, and rang the doorbell at A2. Almost a minute passed. As he started to walk away, he heard the door creak.

A bleary-eyed Muneera frowned at him. Her eyes widened as recognition dawned. "Vincent?"

"Sorry if I woke you," he said, beginning to think this wasn't such a good idea after all. "Do you have a minute?"

She ushered him in, pulling her nightgown around her shoulders. "What's going on?"

He remained standing, facing her, in the narrow hallway that led into her living room. "I guess you haven't heard," he said. "Mr. Shetty walked out last night. They're getting a divorce."

Muneera's delicate nostrils flared, and Vincent took a step back. "And what does that have to do with me?" she said, spitting out each word like a watermelon seed.

"He said he was...he was seeing you."

"He was a customer of mine, if that's what you mean." She folded her arms, still fixing him with her a glare that made him squirm. A bubble of nausea rose up from his stomach, filling his throat with acid.

"How could you, Muneera? He's a married man—"

She laughed, a bitter sound that lashed his skin like a whip. "It may surprise you, but most of my customers are married men. He paid me well and was always gentle with me. And kind, too. That's all that matters."

He tried to speak, but the words remained unformed, choking him as they filled his throat.

She turned away just as he caught a glimpse of the moisture in her eyes. "Go," she said, her voice breaking. "Go back to your perfect marriage and your perfect wife and your perfect job. Stay in your perfect world, and don't cross the door into mine again."

He wanted to apologize, to tell her he was sorry, that he shouldn't have judged her after everything she had told him. Instead, he left, clutching his briefcase.

Vincent frowned when the receptionist told him his wife was on the line. She rarely called him at work. He wondered if she'd been talking to Mrs. Shetty again, and his heart sank as he picked up the phone.

"Guess what?" Her voice brimmed with excitement. "I got the job. They asked me if I could start next Monday."

He sighed with relief. "That's great news. How about we go out to dinner tonight, to celebrate?"

She chuckled, a low, throaty sound that sent his pulse racing. "Spending my money already, are we? Okay, don't be late."

They dined at Salisha, a Mughlai restaurant near Khar Road station. When they got home, Vincent opened a bottle of eighteen-year old Glenfiddich, a wedding gift from one of his cousins. They'd been saving it for a special occasion.

Later, as Diana lay beside him with her head resting on his chest, she told him how happy she was that her life had a purpose again. He brushed a strand of her hair away from his nose, before it could make him sneeze. He thought about his conversation with Muneera, and an iron band tightened around his heart, dispelling the pleasant haze induced by the Scotch and the supple, warm body lying next to him. As if sensing it, Diana rolled over on top of him and gazed into his eyes, a hint of mischief dancing in her own.

"This really has been a perfect day," she whispered. "I won't let anyone—especially my parents—spoil this for me."

Diana began to radiate a glow that filled the room whenever she arrived home from the school. The calls from her parents increased in frequency until one night, as Vincent was reading in the bedroom, he heard her slam the phone.

She flopped onto the bed. He put his book away, bent forward, and began to massage her shoulders, a reflexive habit he'd developed early in their relationship. He saw she wasn't crying, as he'd initially supposed, but that her eyes glittered with rage.

After she calmed down, she told him there was only one thing to do. "We have to sell this flat and give back the money," she said, sitting up in bed and facing him. "It's the only way for us to live our own lives."

A strange numbness began to spread through his arms and legs. "What are we going to do?" he said. "Where will we go?"

"With both of us working, we can find a small place for rent. Maybe even here in Bandra. I know it won't be the same as having our own flat, but let's face it—this isn't really ours, either." He kissed her forehead, knowing she was right.

It took them less than a month to find a two-room rental flat near Santacruz station, convenient to both their jobs. The Bandra flat sold soon after that, requiring just a single advertisement in the *Times of India* classifieds before they were deluged with offers. For the second time that year, Vincent surveyed a living room filled with boxes. He directed the movers to take special care with the furniture, especially Diana's antique roll-top desk that had been a gift from her grandfather. Her parents had been furious when they'd heard the flat had sold, and they refused to take the money. His parents, by contrast, accepted the decision with equanimity. "Probably for the best," his father had said when he'd learned the reason. Finally, when Diana threatened to give the proceeds from the sale to charity, her parents had reluctantly come around.

Vincent took one last look around the flat. "You go check on the movers," he said. "I'll lock up here and be downstairs in a minute."

Muneera's face held no trace of emotion when she answered the door. "Yes?"

"I...we're leaving, and I wanted to say goodbye. I'm sorry about—"

"Goodbye, Vincent," she said and shut the door.

The Deep Blue Sea

THE FAMILIAR RATTLING SOUND made Mario glance up from his desk. Saifi wheeled the cart closer, fumbling with the mail arranged in neat piles. His face broke into a broad grin. The tip of his bulbous nose quivered, reminding Mario of the pet rabbit he had as a child.

"Yes, I have mail for you, Mr. Coutinho." He handed Mario an irregular stack of envelopes. One of them had a different texture—a crisp, heavyweight paper rarely used by Indian companies. With a deliberate movement, Mario removed it from the rest. The top left corner bore a red trident which, on closer examination, turned out to be an interlocked I and U. The rest of the address confirmed the sender as the Office of Graduate Admissions at Indiana University in Bloomington.

There had been many such envelopes in the months after Mario had graduated from St. Boniface College. Like several of his classmates, Mario filled out application forms almost a year in advance, after receiving packets of information from places like Harvard, Columbia, UCLA, Duke, and Carnegie Mellon. Most of the names meant little to him at the time, but he carefully selected them after researching the most popular catalogs and college guides. He sent the completed applications to his cousin Joachim in Chicago, who was more than happy to write checks for the application fees and mail them. Mario offered to repay him once he made it to the States, but Joachim wouldn't hear of it. After all, Joachim said, this is family, and what would Aunty Lily and Uncle Gavin think of him?

The envelopes began to trickle in the following year, soon after the few days of moderate temperatures that passed for winter in Bombay had ended. The letters were polite but regretful. Mario's BSc degree, they said, was insufficient for admission into the graduate program because US colleges didn't recognize the Indian three-year baccalaureate. They encouraged him to apply to their undergraduate program instead or to reapply after he had obtained his Master's degree.

His parents commiserated with him. Mario knew, though, that they were relieved that their son hadn't been snatched from them and whisked off to a land of which they disapproved but had never visited. One of Mario's classmates, who had been accepted to the University of Kentucky, told Mario not to give up, that it was just a matter of finding the right school. Meanwhile, he had to find work. A chance encounter with an uncle's friend landed him a job at Quintera, one of Bombay's leading advertising agencies—a far cry from the research career he'd imagined himself pursuing.

When it was time again, he filled out more applications after swearing Joachim to secrecy. He used his Quintera mailing address so his parents wouldn't intercept the mail—he'd answered enough of their questions the first time around. Once more, the regretful missives had started to appear.

This envelope, however, seemed different. Heavier and larger than he remembered.

He picked up his letter knife and started to slit the envelope with meticulous care, fighting the urge to rip it open with his fingers. Conflicting emotions bubbled up from deep inside him and commenced full battle in his throat. His hands trembled as he extracted the first sheet of paper. He unfolded it, smoothing out the creases as he read. The words danced before his eyes: pleased to inform you...accepted to the graduate program... classes begin August 29...contact the International Students Office on arrival...

A shadow fell across Mario's desk, and he shoved the envelope under a stack of manila folders.

"Mario? I have some good news."

Mario forced an expression of casual indifference and looked up to see his manager hovering nearby. Mr. Ramsay stood with interlocked fingers, bicycling his thumbs in a mannerism that Mario knew well.

"Yes, sir. What is it?"

Mr. Ramsay cleared his throat and adjusted the knot of his flowing red tie. "You remember the Sangam Bio account? The new client we met last week?"

Mario nodded. He'd been impressed by the brief introductory meeting with the biotech company's founder, Selwyn Pinto, although Mario hadn't said much, letting Mr. Ramsay lead the discussion. After all, his boss was the senior account manager while Mario had less than a year of experience as a copywriter.

"I received a call from Mr. Pinto today, and he would like...he insisted...that you pitch the DNA-Max advertising campaign next week."

Mario sat upright, shoving his chair away from the desk as Mr. Ramsay blinked at him. "But sir, you should be the one—"

Mr. Ramsay waved his hands. "I know, I know. This is very odd, indeed. I told Mr. Pinto that, but he was very persuasive. He said that with your background in molecular biology, you understood their business the best. What's more, he wants us to start with a small team—just you, me, and a designer—to keep the cost down. They're still trying to raise additional funding. I wouldn't normally agree to this, but we have to make the client happy."

Mario stood up and grasped Mr. Ramsay's limp, sweaty hand. "Don't worry, sir. I won't let you down."

Mr. Ramsay nodded and extracted his hand from Mario's grip. "I suspect there's another reason Mr. Pinto asked for you. You two are both Goans, isn't that so? Makapaos?"

Mario took a deep breath. "I don't think that has anything to do with it, sir."

Mr. Ramsay stared, his beady eyes looking even smaller behind his thick glasses. "Well, we shall see...you fellows always stick together. We need to come up with a good plan. I'm sure you'll be fine, Mario, but I don't want to lose this account. It could be our biggest one this year. We have to be careful."

Mario walked down the narrow hallway that led to the main conference room. Although the shutters along the glass wall were closed, no light filtered through them, so he opened the door.

He reread the letter one more time—close to the fiftieth, in his estimation, since its arrival the day before. He dropped it on the polished teak table and stepped away, as if it would suddenly burst into flames. He began to pace around the room, hands clasped behind his back.

After a few minutes, he picked up the phone that sat on a wicker stand by the door. "Hema? Do you have some time before the meeting starts? I'm in the conference room."

Mario slumped into a chair after hanging up the phone. He rested his elbows on the table and cradled his head in his hands. As he struggled to come up with a coherent explanation, the faint but unmistakably sweet—almost fruity—scent of jasmine sent his pulse racing.

"What's going on?" Hema closed the door with a soft click.

He raised his head, resisting the overwhelming instinct to take her in his arms. Instead, he pointed to the letter lying on the table. As she read it, her eyes widened. She reached across the table, pressing his hand between hers. "That's great! I'm so happy for you."

The warmth of her skin made his fingers tingle, and he pulled back. "I haven't decided what I'm doing, so don't mention it to anyone as yet."

She raised her perfectly shaped eyebrows. "Haven't decided? Isn't this what you've wanted ever since I've known you?"

He looked into her eyes, searching for answers to questions that remained unasked. "It is. I just have to sort out a few things first. Right now, I don't want anything to interfere with this Sangam Bio project."

She nodded. While she looked over her notes, Mario watched her out of the corner of his eye. A year ago, the decision would have been easy.

They had met on his first day at Quintera, while he was still navigating the rabbit warrens of the office. He ended up in a section with a group of employees gathered in one cubicle, discussing something in front of an enormous computer monitor—the largest he'd ever seen.

As he watched for a brief moment, the young woman at the monitor gesticulated as she pointed out various features of what appeared to be a Maruti Suzuki car speeding down a deserted road. The others nodded and interjected various comments about the angle of the shot, the color temperature, and lighting. Finally, they realized they were not alone, and the woman swung round to face Mario.

"Can I help you with something?"

The color of her eyes struck him at once, holding him captive. He'd expected the deep brown common to most women he knew, but hers seemed to change as he looked, wavering between a golden brown and pale green. He fumbled for words. "I...uh...I'm new here, and I think I got a bit lost. I'm supposed to be working with Mr. Ramsay."

She stood up, and her audience began to disperse. "Oh, that's the other end of the floor, near the copy machine. Come on, I'll show you. I'm Hema Keswani, by the way."

A week later, he was assigned to a project team that included Hema as the lead designer. As they collaborated on the project, he grew to appreciate her creativity and flair for design, but working in close proximity with her had its own challenges.

At last, after the project was done, he asked her out to dinner. Much to his surprise, she accepted.

Soon, they began to see almost as much of each other outside work as they did in the office. Although Mario suspected that Hema's very traditional Sindhi parents would disapprove of their daughter's choice in men, they had never met him. When he asked Hema about it, she simply shrugged. "They wouldn't understand," she said. "In fact, they'd probably forbid me to go out with you. They've been trying to marry me off ever since I graduated."

Eventually, Mario let the issue drop and began to enjoy their forbidden relationship for what it was: an impermanent solution. For a while, he was content with occasional dinners, shopping trips along Colaba Causeway, and simply taking walks along the shoreline that embraced Nariman Point, a few blocks from Quintera's offices. After several months, stolen moments in darkened movie theaters progressed to hurried trysts in dingy hotel rooms. In spite of a level of intimacy he hadn't experienced with his previous, short-lived relationships, Mario had struggled to define exactly what they meant to each other.

Mr. Ramsay coughed as he walked into the conference room, making Mario jump.

As the meeting started, Mario managed to set aside everything else and focus on the task at hand. They outlined their initial plan for the DNA-Max campaign while Mr. Ramsay listened, nodding his head and occasionally interrupting with questions. To Mario's surprise, his manager supported most of their ideas. "Not our traditional approach," he said, polishing his glasses with a perfectly folded white handkerchief. "However, this is a high-tech company founded by a younger generation. They may not respond well to a more conservative campaign. Good work, both of you."

A pink tinge colored Hema's cheeks as an uncomfortable warmth spread through Mario's own. "Thank you, sir. We're confident that it's the right approach. We'll plan three concepts, as usual. We can design one of them around a more conservative strategy, if you like."

After Mr. Ramsay left, Mario continued discussing the campaign with Hema. She attempted to steer the conversation back to his offer from IU, but he shook his head.

"Just a few more days," he said, checking his leather-bound planner. "Let's get together after the pitch meeting next Friday, and I'll explain everything. I promise."

Mr. Ramsay introduced Selwyn Pinto, who greeted Mario as if he were a childhood friend. His companion, Mr. Mehta, had not been present at the initial meeting. The CTO and cofounder of Sangam Bio was a gaunt man with a face that reminded Mario of a brooding vulture. His thinning hair showed touches of gray at the temples, in contrast to Mr. Pinto's well-cropped curls that glistened under the fluorescent light.

"Mr. Ramsay tells me you went to St. Boniface—is that right?" Mr. Pinto leaned forward in his chair across from Mario.

Mario gulped. "Yes, sir. Life Science batch of '93."

Mr. Pinto smiled. "Ah, of course. They didn't have that major when I was there. Chemistry batch of '72. Times have changed, but I'm sure you probably spent as much time in the canteen as you did in class."

Mario, unsure whether an answer would incriminate him, occupied himself by selecting a bottle of Thums Up from the ice bucket at the center of the table. Mr. Pinto went on to describe how he'd spent over ten years working his way up the ranks of a large, multinational biochemicals company in Thana before leaving it to start Sangam Bio in 1990. Although Mario had heard the story before, he listened with polite interest. He couldn't help admiring Mr. Pinto's quiet confidence, the way he commanded attention just by his presence, yet put everyone at ease with a few words and a smile that made him look like a schoolboy.

As Mr. Ramsay proceeded with the preliminaries, Mario wished he could crank up the air-conditioning in the room. He tugged at his collar, gulped a mouthful of his drink, and folded his hands in his lap so the others wouldn't see how much they were shaking. He shot a quick look across the table at Hema. The warmth in her eyes calmed his nerves just a little.

Mr. Ramsay concluded with a recitation of Quintera's impressive client roster—Hindustan Lever's soaps and cosmetics, Maruti Suzuki cars, Britannia bread, and many other household names that failed to elicit more than a head waggle from his guests. With a shaky laugh that sounded like a myna bird, he nodded at Mario and sat down. Wringing his hands, Mario walked to the head of the table, where a collection of concept boards lay against the wall. He hoisted the first one onto the easel.

As he launched into the concept, Mario began to breathe normally again. Soon, he found himself enjoying the spotlight. They had decided to lead with the most conservative approach. This campaign relied heavily on scientific data, with a series of advertisements focused on the technical merits of the product. Mr. Mehta's dark expression lightened and he even asked several questions. In contrast, Mr. Pinto remained silent, steepling his hands in front of his face. His eyes bored into Mario's, but when he moved his hands away, a hint of a smile lingered on his lips. When Mario finished the first concept, Mr. Pinto leaned back in his chair and took a long sip of his drink, clinking the ice cubes in the glass as he swirled it. At the head of the table, Mr. Ramsay fumbled with his tie as he watched Mr. Pinto's reaction. Mario paused, waiting for a question, but Mr. Pinto merely inclined his head in the direction of the remaining boards.

The next concept replaced some of the scientific content with more abstract, flowing graphics that Hema had spent several days tweaking. The layouts added more white space and made effective use of color, but still kept the technical data at the forefront. Mr. Pinto's eyes lit up, but once again he asked no questions, allowing Mr. Mehta to take the lead.

After the discussion waned, Mario returned to the easel and removed the board. He looked around the room. "As you've probably guessed," he said, clasping his hands behind his back, "we've kept our recommended concept for last. We asked ourselves how DNA-Max would be positioned in the market. It's a unique product that's well ahead of its time—there's nothing else out there that can purify DNA, RNA, and protein from the same sample. So we decided that a revolutionary product deserved a revolutionary campaign."

He hoisted the final board onto the easel and pointed to the first quadrant, which contained the advertising mockup. In the cobalt blue color that they'd picked up from the company logo, a bold headline read: "A revolution in biological sample preparation." The rest of the space was blank, except for a small photo of the DNA-Max instrument, surrounded by its multi-hued reagent bottles, in the center. A single line of text at the bottom—"Don't take our word for it. Try it free for thirty days."—was followed by Sangam Bio's phone number.

Mario surveyed the room once again. The deathly silence was broken only by Mr. Ramsay clicking his pen at a furious pace as he waited for Mr. Pinto. Mario forced himself to concentrate on Mr. Pinto as well, denying himself the luxury of a quick look at Hema for reassurance.

After what seemed like an hour, a broad smile spread across Mr. Pinto's face and he rose to his feet. "Excellent!" he said, clapping his hands. "That's exactly the approach we need for this product. Your idea of a free trial will definitely get our customers talking."

Mario exhaled and mopped his forehead. He was about to continue when he saw the frown gathering on Mr. Mehta's face. Mr. Ramsay appeared to ignore it as he reached across the table and shook Mr. Pinto's hand, bubbling with enthusiasm over his team's efforts and how he, Mr. Ramsay, had known all along that they would come up with the perfect campaign.

The rest of the meeting dissolved into a formless blur as Mario finished describing the other marketing pieces on the board and then collapsed into his chair. He barely paid attention to the conversation, letting Mr. Ramsay ramble on about the project timeline and deliverables. The glow in Hema's eyes was the only thing he remembered after they left the room.

*

Mario chewed on the tip of his pen. His head was still reeling from the morning's meeting. The trilling of the phone cut through the haze, like a nariyal-paniwala's knife slicing off the top of a fresh, green coconut. The receptionist announced Mr. Pinto was on the line, and Mario fumbled for a notepad. "Put him through," he said, scribbling on one corner with the recalcitrant pen.

He wondered why Mr. Pinto was calling him and not Mr. Ramsay, who handled all client contact. Maybe there was something to Mr. Ramsay's speculation about makapaos sticking together after all. Still, he'd better take careful notes.

Mr. Pinto's voice sounded a little raspy, like he had a sore throat. After a minute of chitchat about St. Boniface, to Mario's relief, he got down to business.

"I wanted to talk to you about the pitch earlier today," he said, lowering his voice even further so that Mario had to strain to to hear him. "I was very impressed by your presentation and your ideas." He cleared his throat. "In fact, I'd like to offer you a position here at Sangam Bio."

Mario sat upright in his chair and dropped his pen. He tried to retrieve it with his foot as it rolled under the desk.

Without waiting for a response, Mr. Pinto continued. "You would handle all our marketing and work with a freelance designer. At the moment, of course, you would have to do a lot of different tasks. As the company grows, we hope to develop a full marketing team. Eventually, I'd like you to head that effort."

Mario hoped Mr. Pinto couldn't hear his heart thumping over the phone. His mind raced through several possible responses. "I'm...I'm very flattered that you asked me. It sounds like a wonderful opportunity. Can I call you back on Monday and let you know?"

"Of course," Mr. Pinto said. "Take all the time you need. If you're interested in learning more, we can set up a meeting here at the office, and I'll introduce you to our management team."

A twenty-minute ride on a BEST bus filled to capacity, with passengers hanging from the doorways, brought Mario and Hema around Wellington Circle in front of the Regal cinema. They jumped off as the bus slowed down, just beyond the theater's pale yellow façade that marked the start of Colaba Causeway. Hema stole a quick, longing glance at the roadside bookstall that sprawled beside the entrance to Cafe Mondegar. It displayed the latest editions of *Filmfare*, *Stardust*, and other Bollywood magazines, along with the more staid *Times of India* newspaper and *India Today* magazine, carefully arranged on plastic sheeting that covered a portion of the pavement. Behind glass doors in bookcases that rose to twice Mario's height, imported *New York Times* bestsellers jostled for space with cookbooks, comics, and an assortment of pirated paperbacks. Mario enjoyed looking for the latest science-fiction novels every time he visited Colaba's multitude of booksellers, and for a moment he considered allowing them both to indulge in the simple pleasure of browsing the shelves. It would have to wait, though. He grasped Hema's elbow and guided her away from the bookstall.

"Are we going to a movie?" They passed the posters on the side of the Regal as they turned onto Lansdowne Road. A black dinosaur skeleton on a red field dominated the display, and throngs of eager moviegoers jostled each other for a better glimpse at the photographs locked away in glass cases. Mario and Hema often went to a movie on Friday nights, but Mario shook his head.

"Patience," he said, putting an arm around Hema's waist, "is a virtue."

His hand slipped lower, resting for a moment on the delicious curve of her hips. She smacked it away. "You, of all people, should know I have considerably less virtue ever since I met you."

He grinned and kept walking. The road wound past a series of street vendors selling trinkets to eager tourists in the imposing shadow of the Taj hotel across the street. As they approached the ever-present food vendors, Mario's stomach began to growl.

"Are you hungry?"

Hema nodded her agreement, so they stopped at a bhel puri stall. Mario tried to quell his stomach's increasingly loud complaints as he watched the man mix puffed rice with thin strands of sev. Next, he added chopped onions, small chunks of boiled potatoes, and minced green chilies. After tossing the mixture in a cone of newspaper with black salt, jeera, and chaat masala, he drizzled it with the two essential sauces—sweet, tangy tamarind, and spicy coriander with green chili. Finally, he topped off the confection with crisp, deep-fried puris that doubled as convenient scoops. Mario handed the cone to Hema and waited his turn.

They sat on a bench in the paved circle directly in front of the imposing, yellow basalt arch of the Gateway of India. Mario devoured his bhel, leaving little room for conversation, in spite of the expectant look in Hema's eyes. A flock of pigeons bobbed near their feet, hoping for a few wayward crumbs. Ahead of them, a tour group—flashbulbs firing in random confusion—lined up for the ferry ride to Elephanta Island and its famed cave temples carved out of the rocky hillside. A scattering of beggars worked their way through the line of tourists, offering up increasingly morbid tales of woe as they sought out easy targets.

After they'd eaten, Mario led Hema through the Gateway and then to its right, stopping at the stone wall that curved along the harbor. Behind them, a continuous stream of taxis and cars passed through the circular driveway at the entrance to the Taj, disgorging passengers and luggage. Bell boys in crisp navy blue uniforms trimmed with gold brocade vied for attention, each hoping to garner the largest tip.

Hema hoisted herself onto the waist-high wall and sat facing Mario, with her back to the giant disk of the sun low on the horizon. Her hair, liberated by the wind that whipped in from the ocean, flowed around her shoulders as if it had a life of its own. Mario breathed slowly, inhaling her beauty, and placed his hands in her lap. Although the fading light cast her face in shadow, Mario could see the smile in her eyes as she caressed his hand.

"This was where I kissed you for the first time." He leaned forward.

"I remember," she said, her voice dropping to a whisper that he strained to hear over the roar of the waves breaking against the rocks below. "We got some rude comments from those old women walking by." She giggled and pushed the hair out of her eyes. "I can't wait anymore. Tell me what you decided about IU."

Mario sighed. "I was so sure I wanted to pursue graduate studies in the States. That's all I thought about last year. Then I met you, and it's…things are different now." He stopped, trying to collect his thoughts.

Hema's fingers quivered under his own. "What do you mean?"

Mario's heart began to pound against his ribs. He looked down at the tips of his shoes. The rough pavement felt like it was falling away from under his feet. "The thing is…I want us to be together."

She slid down from the wall, breaking contact. "What are you suggesting? That we get married?"

The blood rushed to his cheeks. "Well, yes. I mean…I don't know."

"It's not going to happen. Mario, we've discussed this before. I enjoy what we have, but we both know my parents have other plans for me. In any case, they would throw me out of the house if I even mentioned I was seeing a boy who wasn't Sindhi. Especially one who didn't have business ties to the family."

A throbbing pain spread through Mario's chest. He wanted to argue, to take her in his arms and tell her she was wrong, that they could make it work. Most of all, he wanted to tell her about the job offer from Mr. Pinto and what it could mean for their life together.

Instead, he looked over Hema's shoulder at the rippling streak of the sun's dying rays. They walked away from the rhythm of the waves, fingers entwined, to a taxi that waited at the curb. Mario held the door open for Hema—probably for the last time, he thought, as he slid into the seat. She snuggled close to him, her head resting on his shoulder. Yet it felt like a gulf had opened up between them. They rode in silence for long minutes.

"Why?" he whispered, at last. "Why does it have to be this way?"

Her body stiffened against him, then went limp. "It's always been this way," she said, her voice breaking. He noticed her tears then, glistening on her cheeks in the intermittent glow of the streetlights along Marine Drive.

He put his arm around her, wanting the ride to last forever. "Let's just remember what we have," she said. A sharp retort rose to his lips, but he bit it back. Once again, they lapsed into an uneasy silence until the taxi pulled up at the entrance to the soaring, thirty-story building in Cuffe Parade where Hema lived.

Mario directed the driver to his address and stared at the cars speeding by as the taxi lurched forward. He tried to imagine his world without Hema. She was right about their shared memories. They'd always have those, but memories were a poor substitute for the way he felt when he looked into her eyes, the soft fluttering of her lips on his, the lightness of her touch as she ran her fingers down his chest, the ecstasy of her skin—warm and sweating—against his own.

"You'll have all kinds of American girls chasing after you," she had said, as she'd left the taxi. "You won't miss me at all." Somewhere inside his head, a tiny voice told him she was right, that he'd get over it, that this was just a passing phase. But right now, all he wanted was to find the owner of that tiny voice and beat the shit out of him.

*

The constant buzz of the crowd around Mario was punctuated only by the drone of undecipherable flight announcements. It had been a tearful farewell at the gate, as he'd expected. His mother had clung to him as if he'd been stricken by a fatal disease, refusing to let him go until his father gently pried them apart. After he'd crossed the first security checkpoint, Mario's eyes had scanned the people lined up behind the ramshackle barrier that separated visitors and passengers. Even though the rational part of his brain told him it was futile, he spent several minutes hoping against all reason to spot Hema's face. After the khaki-clad security officers started giving him strange looks, he'd given up and proceeded to the next checkpoint.

Mario peered at the flickering computer monitors overhead while he waited in the passenger lounge, shifting his weight in the squeaky, bright orange plastic seat. He rechecked his tickets, just to be sure. Earlier, at the ticket counter, he'd inquired several times whether his luggage was booked through to Chicago, to the discernible exasperation of the Air India agent. He hoped Joachim would remember to meet him at O'Hare. Mario scarcely remembered what his cousin looked like. During the hour-long phone call the previous night, Joachim had told Mario several times how much he looked forward to seeing him. He'd even offered to drive Mario from Chicago to Bloomington when the time came. Mario, lacking any comprehension of the distance between the two cities, had agreed at once.

A surreal cloak still wrapped the new life awaiting him, and he wondered how long it would take before reality set in. Over the six months that had elapsed since he received the letter, he'd come to realize that Hema would go on with her life, get married to the man her parents had chosen, and the memories that burned so brightly now would fade in time. And when he had walked through that first gate, he had almost convinced himself he'd made the right decision. Still, as he looked at the giant airplane sitting at the gate, the ghostly fingers of doubt caressed his mind, leaving wispy strands of memories that lingered despite his best efforts to brush them away.

An hour later, he gazed out into a sea of clouds tinged with fire from the first rays of the sun. He opened the book he'd brought with him, but the words blurred before his eyes. He eased back in his seat, looked at the tiny plastic rectangle that connected him to the world outside, and let the book fall into his lap. The hum of the engines was strangely comforting as the aircraft climbed higher, heading west over the foam-crested waters of the Arabian Sea.

Solar Power

MOST DAYS, I HATE MY JOB. It wasn't always this way. I used to work in development, designing new solar collectors with a team of enthusiastic engineers. Those were good times: hard work, yes, but everyone was dedicated to the projects. We had minimal interference from management, and that helped even more.

Then my boss, Mr. Rai, decided to move me into sales. I had no previous sales experience, and not even the slightest interest in selling our products instead of making them. But of course that didn't matter to Mr. Rai, who had a penchant for reading—and completely misinterpreting—every trendy management or leadership book he could find. One of them probably gave him the idea that he must shuffle people around every so often to increase productivity.

The phone rings and Dorothy, our receptionist, announces that a Mr. Pesi Daruwala is on the line. I frown as I try to connect the dots in my head. The name sounds vaguely familiar, but I can't put a face to it. I decide to accept the call, more out of curiosity than anything else. I hope it isn't a sales call, some other poor slob like myself hoping to boost his commission before the end of the quarter.

"Peter? Peter Braganza?" The voice is crisp, clear, with a slight twang. He turns the t in my name to a soft d, indicating he's probably from the States.

"Yes, this is Peter." I emphasize the t.

"You may not remember me, but we were in college together," he says. Definitely an American accent. I've never been to the States, but I've watched enough Hollywood movies in my lifetime to recognize the considerable variation from the traditional Parsi inflection. "Physics batch of '86. I went to the States after that, got my PhD in double-E at a place called Purdue, in Indiana."

Images come swirling into my mind like pages of a newspaper whipped up by the wind. A tall, skinny, very introverted Parsi boy with a pencil-thin mustache. Never said more than a few words to me and always seemed to be studying while I hung out in the canteen with my friends, smoking, eating, drinking tea. Discussing politics, girls, and cricket, not always in that order.

"Yes, I do remember you." I lean back in my swivel chair with a degree of caution. It has a tendency to tip over backwards if you push its limits too far. "How long have you been back in Bombay?"

"About a month," he says. Now I realize what I remember best about Pesi isn't Pesi himself but his cousin Roshna. A pale girl with finely sculpted cheekbones, wavy shoulder-length hair, and large, warm eyes who turned all the boys' heads, mine included, whenever she walked into the canteen. Strangely enough, even though Pesi had been my classmate for months—there were just under a hundred of us in the Physics batch of '86—it was Roshna who introduced me to him.

"Listen," he says, "I'd like to catch up when you have a chance. I've been in touch with a few of our classmates, and they told me to consult you."

As I shoot a glance at the clock on the wall, there's a tentative tap on my door. Without waiting for a response, as usual, Mr. Rai walks in. I raise a hand, and he nods, seating himself across from me. I turn back to the phone, twisting the cord with one finger. "I'd be happy to get together," I say, opening my appointment book. "How about lunch on Friday? We can meet here at the office, if you like. There are quite a few restaurants nearby." Pesi confirms. I give him the address, hang up, and finally look at Mr. Rai, who is playing with the collar of his pale yellow, polyester-blend shirt.

"A new client?" he asks, leaning forward. I sense the eagerness in his voice, like a dog whining at the scent of a rabbit.

I shrug, not wanting to get his hopes up. Besides, it's none of his business anyway. Okay, maybe it is his *business*, but you know what I mean. "I'm not sure, sir. Old college friend. He wants to discuss a project."

Mr. Rai's bloodshot eyes brighten at first but then resume their normal unfocused stare. "Well, if you take him to lunch, don't charge it to the company, you hear? I don't want to be paying for your friends to eat lunch."

I reassure him that lunch will be entirely my responsibility. He rambles on for a while about how he paid for every lunch himself when he started the company, and how we should all develop a good sense of fiscal discipline. From there, he takes off on several tangents, touching on the dangers of fried food, why a daily morning cleansing of the sinuses helps to fight infections, and how to tell which street vendors between Fort and Flora Fountain are selling fake electronics (they all are).

As over thirty minutes tick by, he folds his hands in his lap and gets to the point. "I've been looking at the numbers for this quarter, and they're down from last year by almost twenty percent." He removes his thick, square-framed glasses and polishes them with the tail of his shirt, then bends to scratch a big toe that protrudes from his worn leather sandals.

He looks back up at me and his bushy eyebrows connect, forming a black caterpillar above his nose. "This isn't good, Peter. We must improve our sales soon. Otherwise, we will need to tighten our belts here at Solindia."

I begin to tell him why sales are down, but he notices the clock, realizes he's late for a meeting, and rushes off, almost knocking over the chair. I stand up, stretch, and walk around my office a few times, watching the incessant snarl of traffic along Sandhurst Road twenty floors below.

That evening, as the bus winds its away through the dusty, clamorous streets of Pydhonie, I wonder how much Pesi's life has changed since we graduated and whether he's as dissatisfied with the way things turned out as I am. One thing's for sure, he's not stuck in a job where he doesn't belong, hanging on only because of a paycheck. Come to think of it, I don't know if he has a job at all. Why is he back in Bombay after all these years? It seems odd, but there must be a good explanation. I'll have to wait a few days to find out.

Friday finds me escorting Pesi down the road to Cafe Simple, a dilapidated restaurant just a few minutes from the office. It serves a decent assortment of Mughlai food, and the prices would satisfy even Mr. Rai's frugal standards. We order a bottle of Golden Eagle to start with while we peruse the hand-written menu on a blackboard. It hangs on a faded wall where the paint has peeled away in spots, leaving irregular marks that my eyes always connect to form patterns, much like children do with clouds.

Pesi looks, oddly enough, very much like I remember him from our days at St. Boniface. He's a few kilos heavier, possibly, but otherwise seems to have survived the passage of ten years very well. I glance down at the slight bulge above my belt and decide that Pesi has definitely come off the better in that contest.

The beer arrives and Pesi pours it into glasses that are chipped along the rims. I wonder if that will bother him after living in the States, but he makes no mention of it and raises his glass to mine.

We toast St. Boniface, within whose rough-hewn, Indo-Gothic stone walls we formed enough memories to last a lifetime. It doesn't take long for us to slip into reminiscing about the days we spent there, and I discover that somewhere along the way, Pesi has turned into a remarkable conversationalist. He regales me with colorful accounts of his life as a graduate student at Purdue as if it were just yesterday. In turn, I feed him information on a few of our classmates with whom I've kept in touch over the years.

The food arrives, steam rising in hazy clouds. Pesi looks at his plate of mutton biryani, with its accompanying saucer of pickle and a crisp but very oily papad. "This is what I missed the most," he says, waving a hand. "This and cricket. You can't get any coverage of cricket there, unless you have this new satellite service. And even then, only one provider offers just a few matches each year."

"What about baseball?" I ask, having recently seen *The Fan* at the Strand in Colaba.

Pesi shrugs. "Yeah, I watched a fair amount of baseball on TV. I even became a Red Sox fan when I moved to Boston for a job. Fenway is an awesome ball park, and I got to catch quite a few games there. It's not the same, though."

I mumble my agreement through a mouthful of rice saturated with lamb curry, savoring the astringent combination of tamarind and vinegar. As much as I enjoy dwelling on our college days, I'm still curious about why Pesi is here. As he breaks a piece of papad and scoops up some of the pickle, he reads the question in my eyes. "I guess I should explain why I called you."

I nod as I chew on a particularly gristly chunk of lamb.

"You're familiar with the dakhmas—the Towers of Silence— near Malabar Hill?"

I almost choke on the lamb and have to take a large gulp of my beer. I remember the Towers well.

I was about five or six years old, visiting my cousin, Sam, who lived a few minutes from the Towers in a high-rise Malabar Hill building. We were playing with the latest toys his parents had bought on their annual shopping trip to Singapore, when we heard his mother screaming like the forces of hell had been unleashed. We ran into the living room and found her standing in the open balcony, yelling for the servant and pointing to something on the floor.

The servant came running into the room and tried to pacify my aunt, but apparently, that just made things worse. Finally, she bent over, picked up whatever it was on the floor and headed back to the kitchen, leaving my aunt to scream all the more. We led her into the living room and got her to sit down on the sofa, still having no idea what all the fuss was about. At length, she calmed down enough to fix herself a large gin and tonic, which helped her respond to our insistent questions.

"It was a finger," she said, shuddering as she lowered her glass. "A human finger. Those bloody vultures must have dropped it right into the balcony."

My cousin and I resumed playing, both accepting that human fingers fell from the sky all the time, and agreeing there was no reason to make such a fuss about it. When I returned home that day and described the incident to my older sister, she explained the traditional Parsi funeral rites to me. It all seemed a bit odd at the time but, since then, I must admit I've never given it much thought.

Pesi continues to sip his beer, watching me with a hint of concern. "Yes," I say, "I'm familiar with the Towers of Silence."

He drains his glass and refills it from the amber bottle, signaling for another. "While I was away, my parents were updating me on a serious problem that's affecting the Parsi community here in Bombay. In fact, it's happening in many of the bigger cites—all across India."

He pauses to pick a bone out of his mouth and sets it on the table beside his plate. He gives me a shy grin, looking very much like the Pesi I knew ten years ago. "I'd forgotten about the mutton here having bones in it. Anyway, the vultures are housed in a sanctuary that surrounds the Towers, but they're not caged. They're free to roam the area."

And drop body parts into the balconies of unsuspecting neighbors.

"Unfortunately," Pesi continues, "they're dying out. Their population in Bombay has been reduced by ninety percent from what it was a decade ago. Efforts to breed them in captivity are failing."

I frown. "Dying out?"

He nods. "Not from natural causes, though. There's a drug called diclofenac that's being used to treat cattle. It's relatively cheap, easily available, and very effective in controlling infections. Unfortunately, it's also lethal to vultures."

"How many vultures are left?"

"Just a handful," he says, shoveling biryani into his mouth as if he hadn't eaten for days. "In a year, maybe even less, they too will be gone."

An ugly image forms in my mind and I try to wash it away with the beer. "How long does it take the vultures to...um—"

"Dispose of a corpse?" He wipes a few errant grains of rice from his chin. "When the flock was at full strength, they could tackle a single body in an hour or two. Strip it down to the bones. Now, it could take several days, even a week."

I shudder. "I've always wondered why Parsis don't just cremate their dead."

He shakes his head. "Fire is sacred to us," he says, "as are the other elements—earth, water, and air. When life leaves a person's body, what is left is considered unclean. To cremate a body would mean defiling the holy fire. It's not an option. Neither is burial, for that matter."

"So what's your plan?" I'm still trying to figure out why he chose to contact me above all people. Not that I don't have something of an interest in the funerary practices of various cultures, but I'm sure another Parsi would be far more helpful in this situation.

He toys with the food on his plate, then puts his fork down. "There's one solution that may be acceptable to the community. It would satisfy both the traditionalists and the more progressive faction. Part of the dedication rite is to offer the body to the sun. At Purdue, I worked with a lab studying the accelerated decay of organic matter when exposed to solar radiation."

Wheels are beginning to turn in my head, and I don't like where they're taking me.

Pesi drains the rest of his beer, burps with gusto, and wipes his mouth with a satisfied sigh. "Basically, they found that concentrated solar radiation increases the normal rate of decomposition substantially. So I thought, why not apply the same principle to our problem? And, of course, that's why I called you."

My head begins to spin, and it's not from the beer. "Let me get this straight. You want to build a solar collector to decompose dead people."

Pesi smiles, then mimes a gun pointing at me with one hand. "Bingo!" he says—another one of those American expressions I don't quite get. "Actually, it's more than that. I'm setting up a business to manufacture, sell, and install these collectors at dakhmas all over India. And I'd like you to join me."

I nod to the waiter, and he brings over another Golden Eagle. After emptying half my glass, I look at Pesi, who's sitting back in his chair wearing a triumphant smile. "Are you serious? I mean, you really want to go into business doing this?"

He leans forward, elbows resting on the table. "Absolutely. I'd like you to handle the design and oversee the manufacturing. I'll run the company and, of course, work with the local Parsi panchayats to get the system adopted."

"How do you know they'll go for this?"

He sighs. "It won't be easy. Zoroastrianism goes back a long way. It's older than Hinduism or Judaism, and these traditions have survived all this time because there's been a dedicated group of followers keeping them alive through the centuries. But I've already talked to a few members of the panchayat informally, and I can tell you that they're definitely listening. After all, the alternative is burial or cremation—and nobody wants to do that."

I wait for him to go on, but he looks at me, expecting a response. I shake my head. "I need some time to think about this."

He laughs. "Of course. I don't expect you to decide right away. Here's my number." He thrusts a business card at me. "Just give me a call when you make up your mind."

Another conversation with Mr. Rai circles around the point for an hour before he gets to his plans for "austerity measures." He assures me that my job is secure, but several of my salespeople will be affected. It's been three days since my lunch with Pesi, and as outlandish as his scheme sounded at first, is it really more ridiculous than sticking around in a dead-end job, with a boss from another planet, and a company with no sense of direction?

Of course, I'd be lying if I said the financial implications didn't scare me. It's not easy to walk away from a steady paycheck. Being single and renting a tiny flat helps, though. I've managed to build a decent savings account that will help make the decision easier.

I fumble in my wallet for the business card and retrieve it with fingers that tremble just a little.

"Pesi? This is Peter. Let's talk. I'll meet you after work today."

We celebrate over drinks at a bar in Churchgate as the waves of humanity outside clog the streets on their way to torrid train rides home. Inside the bar, it's refreshingly cool— several window air conditioners hum as Indian classical music provides an unobtrusive backdrop to the conversation. These two features alone point to the status of the place as a notch above the others scattered throughout the area. When the bill arrives, I notice that Pesi leaves a generous tip.

Back home, I study the folder of documents Pesi has given me. It takes just under an hour for me to calculate the dimensions and sketch out a rough blueprint of the solar collectors we'll need. We figured out the process is going to be slower—three or four days, depending on the weather, compared to a few hours with the vultures—but, as Pesi said, the panchayat has little choice.

Finding the raw materials for the collectors at a reasonable price is going to be the first hurdle, but with my contacts in the industry, it shouldn't be an insurmountable problem. Pesi has enough capital set aside, it appears, to manufacture several prototypes, and we can fund full-scale production with the help of an investment group his father runs. After a while, I put the papers away and drift off to sleep, visions of giant vultures circling a row of corpses drifting through my head.

The next day I give notice at Solindia. Mr. Rai's face registers shock at first, especially when I tell him I don't have another position lined up. Secretly, though, he seems somewhat relieved. Now he won't have to come up with a creative way to get rid of me. I offer the customary two weeks, and although he presses me for more time, reasons, ways he can change my mind, I stick to my original plan.

The two weeks drift by in a strange, nonlinear haze of activity. Behind it all, I alternate between sheer exhilaration and moments of sudden, gut-wrenching panic. The first day that I wake up and realize I don't have to rush off to work disorients me. It's like time has stopped and I'm the only one not affected, walking through a universe populated by people who stand frozen in comical poses. I manage to shower and dress all the same, deriving some small comfort from the routine. That evening, I decide that a walk will help me clear my head and prepare me for the next morning, when Pesi has managed to secure a meeting with the Parsi panchayat.

My building is a few minutes away from Wilson College, behind the considerably more expensive ones that face Chowpatty beach and the ocean beyond. I walk at a brisk pace, enjoying the all too brief respite from the day's oppressive humidity that is offered by the sun sinking below the waves. I arrive at an intersection where I can blend in with the hordes that cross Marine Drive. We move as a single unit—with an efficiency born of organized chaos—before the light changes.

Along a stretch of the beach sprawls a jumbled collection of food vendors who serve a variety of items designed to seduce even the most reluctant palate. Most of them start their day just before sundown, when the area comes alive with men, women, and children from all walks of life and all parts of Bombay.

My favorite is a samosa vendor, whose food stall bears the name Jai Jawan. Victory to the soldier, appropriate for a man who lost a leg defending the Indian border against Pakistani incursions in two major wars. I greet him, and a smile stretches across his wrinkled face to reach eyes that speak of a full, vigorous life.

The steam coming off the samosa burns the roof of my mouth and I blow on it before taking the next bite. As I leave the food stall and head for the open beach, the sound of the waves filling my ears, I realize a sense of freedom that I haven't felt in a long time. Among the alternating hiss and roar of the ocean, and the squawking of the gulls searching for food scraps in the sand, I find a stillness that soaks deep through my skin, saturating my body. I know I have made the right decision.

Pesi and I sit across a battered folding table from three Parsi gentlemen who are considerably advanced in years. They peer at us, each from behind a pair of thick glasses perched on hawkish noses, and bob their heads, reminding me, oddly enough, of the carrion scavengers we are here to discuss.

As agreed, I let Pesi do most of the talking. In a rare show of deference to my presence, the meeting is conducted in English, rather than the peculiar form of accented Gujarati unique to Bombay's Parsi population.

Pesi outlines his proposal, and the other men let him talk without interruption. He exudes a forcefulness and confidence that I don't remember from our days in college. I watch the men as he speaks. They're focused on Pesi, their eyes following his every gesture, but I can't read any emotion as I scan their faces. Pesi wraps up his presentation and sits back in his chair, inviting questions.

Sarosh, the oldest and the leader of the panchayat, is the first to speak. "This will be a difficult change for us," he says in a voice that rises in pitch at the end of the sentence. He adjusts his glasses. "Yet it is the first alternative I've heard that will allow us to preserve something of our traditions."

"I'm not so sure about that," says the man next to Sarosh, whom Pesi introduced earlier as Rustum Jeejeebhoy. "It is certainly very different from offering the body to the vultures for disposal."

"Keep in mind, Rustum," says Sarosh, "that the ultimate method is the same. The vultures merely hasten the process that is begun by the sun. What Pesi proposes will accomplish the task as well, but it will take a little longer."

"How do these collectors work?" Rustum asks. Pesi turns to me, and I suck in a mouthful of air through my teeth.

"It's a simple principle," I say. "They act like a large mirror, focusing the sun's rays onto an object placed at a precise point, the focal length. At the company where I worked previously, we used this method to build solar cookers that are being distributed in many Indian villages now. Of course, the collectors that we're discussing here will not be as tightly focused, so there's no danger of…of anything catching fire."

The third man, Behram, has remained silent, but now directs a stern look at me. "And what if there's no sun?"

My heart begins to sink. He's found the weak link in our chain of logic, the one issue Pesi and I debated the longest.

Pesi jumps in, sensing my hesitation. "We have an optional attachment," he says, "that stores the sun's energy in batteries. On cloudy days, the batteries can be discharged through a resistance coil embedded in the metal bed that is used to hold the body. It will heat the bed to achieve the same rate of decomposition as that from solar radiation alone." He pauses, shooting a quick look at me.

Don't say it. I will him to stop. But he doesn't.

"In fact," he continues, as I groan inside, "we can even adjust the resistance coil to provide a higher temperature—high enough for complete breakdown within two or three hours. With a different enclosure, of course."

In the heavy silence that follows, I can almost hear their thoughts. Sarosh is the first to get it.

"Impossible!" he shouts, his gray eyebrows dancing up to meet the brim of his fez-like cap. "You are referring to cremation. We cannot accept that."

Pesi holds up a hand, as the other two men voice their protests. "It would not involve any use of fire. The heat is generated strictly by stored electricity, so there's no flame. But, as I said, this is an optional feature that we can provide. It will greatly accelerate the process, but if you wish, we will stick to the original plan when we design the prototype."

He manages to calm the group down. In a few moments, he steers the discussion back on track. I can see why he's appointed himself the point of contact with prospective clients. Besides the obvious advantage of being a Parsi—even though I'm not really sure how he feels about his faith—he has a gift for guiding conversations in precisely the direction he wants.

It's something I know doesn't come easily to me, despite my years of working in sales at Solindia.

"How soon can you make one of these prototypes?" Sarosh asks me.

"We have the final design and some contract workers committed to the project. They can deliver a test unit within two weeks."

Sarosh nods and turns to Pesi. "You will take care of the installation?"

"Yes, of course," Pesi says, his gaze sweeping the room. "Mr. Braganza will train me, and I will install the unit under the panchayat's supervision."

Sarosh settles back in his chair, resting his chin on his hands. The discussion continues, and once again I'm impressed by Pesi's easy manner. He almost has them smiling like schoolboys being told their class has just been canceled.

After a while, the conversation switches to Gujarati for a few moments, and I look down at the table. Sarosh stands up. "Thank you for coming today. We will debate the proposal with the full panchayat this evening and let you know our decision tomorrow."

We shake his hand and gather up our materials. As we walk through the door, Pesi nudges me and gives me a thumbs-up sign. I exhale, letting my body slump into its natural position.

That night, I return to the beach at Chowpatty, unable to sleep. The strains of Hindi film music blend with the shouts of the food vendors, and the aroma of fried onions and greens beckons to me. A pav bhaji vendor hands me a serving wrapped in old newspapers, and I leave him the change from my twenty-rupee note. He thanks me with a look of surprise, offering a brief namaste as I walk away. Although the crowds are thinning at this hour—almost midnight—there are still enough people that I have to fight my way through them. No children or families, who are all in bed, but there are college students and businessmen, taxi cab drivers and off-duty policemen. The maalishwalas are doing business as usual, pressing and kneading sore muscles with skilled fingers. I debate whether a trip to a bar would do me good, but then decide simply to sit on the warm sand and finish the last of my meal. Around the curve of the bay to my right, the lights of Marine Drive glitter like the necklace after which they are commonly named. Ahead, the waves continue to roll in, white crests glowing in the deep indigo of the sea.

Early the next morning, the phone interrupts my dreams. Pesi tells me that the panchayat voted to proceed with the plan. And so our adventure begins. The day fills with more calls and a trip to the manufacturing facility in Sewri, a dark, smelly, industrial sector just northeast of metropolitan Bombay. I hand over blueprints, discuss every detail with the project manager, and leave with a flutter of excitement in my stomach.

We rode the wave for almost ten years, installing collectors in the largest cities in India. Pesi and I worked well together, as it turned out, and our business thrived, making sure that we could look forward to a decent retirement. Then it all went downhill as quickly as it grew. A new breeding program for vultures in captivity began to succeed. Today, the birds are back at the Malabar Hill dakhma and those in many other cities.

We haven't given up, though. We diversified the company to encompass several other applications of solar collectors, and we even have a thriving solar panel business that is gaining government support in rural areas where conventional sources of electricity are scarce. Last week, I received a call from Mr. Rai, whose company was losing more money each quarter even after increasing austerity measures. He proposed that we buy out what was left of Solindia. I thanked him, wished him well, and hung up.

Bhel Plaza

AMIT STOOD MOTIONLESS, savoring the blend of salt air and the rich, velvet aroma of the roasting corn on the cob next door. His neighbor, Subash, fanned the flames of a charcoal stove, making Amit cough as the smoke blew into his face. He adjusted the thin, metal-rimmed glasses on his nose. They had a habit of slipping down too far, lubricated with sweat even as the sun dipped lower and a gentle breeze wafted in from the ocean. He sometimes feared his glasses would drop into the kettle of bubbling oil, in which he now fried a batch of samosas. Soon, the crowds would be gathering at his stall as another evening began at Girgaum Chowpatty beach.

He scooped the samosas onto a tray lined with newspaper, tilted his head, and stretched. The pain from his injury fought back, as it always did when he taxed his muscles too far beyond their limits. Not that stretching would be considered an exertion by a younger man, like Subash. Little more than a boy, Subash often joked about Amit's age, but Amit knew the banter hid a deep, quiet respect. In the two years he'd known Subash, the boy had grown closer to him than his own sons, who were scattered across the country with their families—gone and mostly forgotten.

For the next few hours, Amit thought about little beyond keeping a steady supply of food flowing. He hobbled from the counter to the fryer and back, refilling trays of samosas and vada pav, making sure the containers of chutney were stocked, and dipping into the large, thermocol-lined ice chest for sodas and bottled water as the crowd swelled. As midnight approached, Amit sank onto the solitary cushioned barstool that rested on a piece of plywood. It was a luxury forsaken by most of the vendors in the muddled community of stalls that sprawled across the beach, like colorful pieces of garbage washed up by the tide.

"Arrey, Subash," he said as he polished his glasses with the end of his kurta. "She did not stop by today."

Subash glanced across the counter that separated their stalls. His white, stiff-collared Western-style shirt sported a few rust-colored stains from the mixture of chili powder, salt, and lemon that he rubbed into the corn. "Old man," he said, flashing an even-toothed grin, "she has grown tired of you at last."

Amit clucked his tongue. "Why would she be tired of me, you stupid boy? I have many stories yet to tell her. You wait and see. One day she is going to be a famous writer. Then everyone will read my stories, in India and all over the world."

Subash nodded, running his fingers through his hair as he peered into the mirror that hung on the flimsy wall behind Amit. "Yes, Amitbhai, everyone will read your stories. They will hear all about the wars and how you protected our borders from the Pakistanis for all those years. Then, thank God, I won't be the only one who has to listen to them day after day." He roared with laughter, clutching his sides, then swerved to avoid the potato that Amit flung at him.

"Don't worry, Amitbhai." Subash fanned his stove, making it crackle and spit angry orange sparks. "I'm sure she'll come tomorrow."

The sun hovered at its peak in a cloudless sky when Amit rose the next day. He reached for the crutch that leaned against the whitewashed wall. As he raised himself off the bed, he realized his glasses weren't on the wooden nightstand where he placed them every night. Fighting a sudden stab of panic, he fumbled under his pillow. At last he found them, mercifully unbroken, wedged between the thin mattress and the headboard. He'd fallen asleep with them on, he remembered, and must have taken them off at some point during the night. As he balanced them on his nose, he longed for the perfect vision he had during his army days.

Amit filled a battered kettle with tepid water that trickled from the kitchen faucet. He heated it on the gas stove—a gift from his oldest son—and rummaged in the olive-green refrigerator for some of the left-over food he'd brought home earlier that morning. It had been a good night. Most of his food had sold by one o' clock, as the first round of affluent drunks began staggering home from the bars and combed the beach looking to satisfy their hunger.

As he sipped his tea, hot enough to numb his tongue, he wondered if he would see Nancy today. She usually came by as he was setting up, before the evening rush. It wasn't like her to miss two days in a row.

He had first met Nancy Sequeira a few months earlier when she visited his stall and ordered a plate of samosas with an extra serving of tamarind chutney. She soon won him over with her bright, inquisitive eyes and incessant questions. No one else, not even his own family, had taken such an interest in the particulars of Amit's life. Nancy filled a void in his solitary existence, like the daughter he never had. He learned that she had a day job in nearby Girgaum as a legal secretary but spent her nights working on her first novel. Amit still found it hard to imagine that anyone would want to write about him. When she mentioned the idea, he laughed, thinking it was all a joke.

But Nancy persisted, asking him for details about a past he often tried to forget, all the while weaving together the coarse threads of the life he left behind. He wondered if anyone would read her novel, but she assured him it was going to be very popular, a bestseller. Even Subash, for all his joking, had said it would make Amit famous one day.

Amit sighed as he washed the greasy residue from his fingers. He sank into the armchair in the confined, sparsely furnished space that served as a living room and immersed himself in the newspaper his neighbor left outside Amit's door every morning. After flipping through a few pages of the local news, he wondered if he had enough supplies stashed away underneath the counter of his stall. If not, he would have to send one of the errand boys, who served many of the vendors at Chowpatty, on a trip to the market.

Amit arrived as the miniature carnival was getting started on the beach. The workers scurried across the warm sand as brightly lit merry-go-rounds began their hesitant motion and Bollywood songs blared through speakers lashed to nearby posts. His right shoulder seized up when he finally reached his stall, and he let go of his crutch. Even with the special base attached to the end of his crutch, walking across the sand required an effort that left him taking deep, shuddering breaths. He sank down on the barstool, kneading his shoulder.

Within an hour, the gathering crowd once again left him little time to attend to his comfort. As he embraced the familiar routine, he began to feel better. He even responded to Subash's gentle taunts with a vigor that made Subash laugh all the more.

As he filled a large order of samosas, adding servings of both tamarind and coriander chutneys, he saw Nancy walking across the sand, taking careful, even steps. Unlike most of the other Goan women who visited Amit's stall, Nancy wore a classic salwar kameez—her signature outfit at work. The subdued, earthy tones reflected the color of the sand, and gained some levity from the bright red dupatta draped around her neck.

"Namaste, Amitbhai," she said, folding her hands. "I missed you yesterday, but we took on a new client at the office this week. By the time I was done, I had just enough energy to make it home."

He bowed and returned her greeting, his face lighting up like a child opening his first bag of fireworks for Diwali. He handed an order of vada pav wrapped in newspaper to a customer at the far end of the counter and began preparing a plate of samosas for Nancy.

As he filled the next few orders, they chatted about little things—the weather, her latest shopping spree in the fancy new mall at Gamdevi, Amit's recent telephone conversation with his oldest son in Bangalore. After Nancy finished eating, she fished out her hand-held tape recorder from the depths of the large satchel that dangled off one shoulder. Amit's eyes wandered to the embroidered cross, studded with glittering sequins, that stood in stark relief against the woven jute fabric.

"So what stories do you have for me today?" She fiddled with the recorder, adjusting the controls before she pressed the red button.

Amit smiled as he wiped his hands on a dishrag. "Today, Nancy memsahib, I would like to ask you a question instead. If you will permit it." He opened a Limca, inserted a straw, and handed the bottle to her after wiping the condensation from it.

She gave him a timid smile in return. "I suppose it's only fair. You've told me so much about your life. What would you like to know?"

"I served in the first war before you were born and the second when you were just a child. Tell me, what is your first memory of it?"

Her eyes searched the faded blue wall behind him. "I don't remember much of what happened in '71—I was seven years old—but there's one incident I'll never forget.

"At the time, we were living in a flat near Mazagaon Docks. One night, the radio began to broadcast an emergency bulletin. A squadron of Pakistani planes had been spotted heading toward Bombay harbor. A minute later, the sirens went off, announcing a citywide blackout."

Amit nodded and closed his eyes for a moment. He could almost feel the frenzied activity around him as the alerts rang out over the speakers that hung at a variety of angles from posts throughout the barracks.

"In a few seconds, my parents turned off all the lights in the flat and shut the windows. We heard the police shouting as they patrolled the area, making sure everyone was complying with the blackout order. The street lamps went out moments later. All I saw were some flickering candles in the flats across from us." She paused and took a long sip from her Limca. Amit opened his eyes and caught a glimpse of the naked terror in hers.

"It's okay, Nancy memsahib," he said, as she put the bottle down on the counter. "You don't have to tell me."

She held up a hand as she continued. "I still remember wondering what would happen if our building was bombed. Would I hear a loud explosion, or would I simply be killed right away? I started describing various scenarios to my brothers, but they smacked me on the head and told me not to be an idiot.

"I climbed onto the bed near the window, peering up at the sky. I thought maybe I'd catch a glimpse of the Pakistani planes. As I looked out, a faint glow lit up the sidewalk below. A loud crash and the tinkle of broken glass made me jump. With a huge thud, something fell on the floor less than a meter away from me. I heard curses from the street and someone screaming *batti bund karo*—turn off the light!"

Amit leaned forward, resting an arm on the counter. "Go on," he whispered.

"I jumped off the bed as my parents came running into the room. 'Are you children okay?' my father asked. He picked me up and carried me across the room. 'Those idiots—they hit the wrong window. It must have been the flat above us.'

"We remained in the dark for over an hour, listening to the radio. I stayed away from the windows. I could see bright flashes of what I thought was lightning, but my father told me it was anti-aircraft fire. Later, we found out the Pakistani planes never got near Bombay."

As Nancy finished her story, Amit's hands were shaking. He had been stationed at the northwest border during that war, although most of the action had taken place across the country, to the east. The surrender of Pakistani forces led to celebration of India's biggest military victory. It resulted in the formation of a new nation, the People's Republic of Bangladesh, from what had been East Pakistan. With a shock, he realized the incident Nancy described must have occurred only days before the injury that ended his service.

"I have to get home now, Amitbhai." Nancy shifted the weight of the satchel on her shoulder, then smiled. "I'll see you tomorrow, I promise. Back to our normal routine, okay?"

He nodded and waved as she walked away. He leaned against the counter, covering his ears but unable to shut out the sounds of the artillery fire that echoed in his head.

When Nancy started her tape recorder the next evening, she asked Amit about his first few months in Bombay.

"After my injury and discharge, I was offered resettlement by the ministry of defense. I chose to move to Bombay since I had some cousins living here, but I had not been in touch with them at all during the war. Later, I found out they had moved away after their parents died in a car accident."

Nancy listened while she ate, interjecting an occasional question as Amit continued. Sweat trickled down his forehead, the heat getting to him more than usual that day. His phantom leg itched as if it were covered in red ants, and he struggled against the urge to scratch at the stump.

He'd acquired the food stall through a provisional license granted to him by the Bombay Municipal Commission. It was all part of the resettlement package, the ministry of defense official said. A chance for him to begin a new life after serving his country through two wars.

At first, he'd been terrified in a way that he never was during his time in the service. After all, what did he know about running a food stall, especially in a strange city?

The first night, he slept on a blanket behind the stall. Although the resettlement included a month's free accommodation at a hostel for retired servicemen, Amit feared someone would steal his supplies during the night.

After a few nights of camping out on the beach without incident and striking a bargain with the policemen who made their leisurely rounds in the early morning, Amit decided he'd sleep better in a real bed. He took the last bus back to the hostel, arriving just after two in the morning. Since he was a guest, he made do with a lumpy mattress on a cot in one of the common rooms, along with another two dozen residents. A privileged few had private rooms, but Amit didn't mind. It reminded him of the army barracks.

Gradually, Amit began to get used to the hostel even though he was gone most of the night, unlike the others. His companions spent their time playing cards, swapping war stories, and watching the run-down television set in the mess hall. It sputtered and flickered through broadcasts on the solitary Doordarshan channel that it received over the rooftop antenna, for the hostel had no cable connection. Amit understood now that cable had become all the rage. The thick black ribbons snaked across terraces and rooftops throughout

Bombay, forming a precarious network that brought the world to the city.

As he neared the end of his complimentary stay, he began to panic. He had pored over the newspaper every day, looking for a place to rent that would not exhaust his monthly pension. He begged and pleaded with the manager of the hostel to give him another month, even offering to pay, but the retired colonel remained firm. The rules, he said, allowed for no exceptions.

Then a stroke of luck brought a large, gruff man to Amit's stall two days before the month was up. He introduced himself as Mr. Lalwani and struck up a conversation with Amit as he plucked at a vada pav with stubby fingers. He was a landlord, he said, managing several buildings in Girgaum. When he heard Amit was an ex-serviceman, he promptly offered him a two-room flat in a building off Marine Drive, across from Chowpatty beach. Amit hadn't even considered the old but astronomically priced buildings in his search, but Mr. Lalwani said he'd cut the rent to an amount that was little over half Amit's pension. Amit protested at first, unable to accept the generosity of a stranger, but Mr. Lalwani insisted. "My son is serving in Kashmir," Mr. Lalwani said, grasping Amit's hand. "Every day, I worry about him getting killed, wondering whether he will ever return home. You will do me an honor by renting this flat, Amitbhai."

"And so, my life in Bombay began in earnest," Amit said, offering Nancy another samosa plate and waving away her ten-rupee note. She thanked him with a smile. "After more than twenty years, I am still paying the same rent, and Lalwani sahib is my closest friend. He now owns many buildings in Girgaum and other parts of the city, so I am sure he is very comfortably situated. Yet he calls me every week to see how I am getting along, and he visits every month."

Nancy wiped a few crumbs from her chin with a swift movement. "What about his son? Is he still in Kashmir?"

Amit shook his head, pushing back the stark images that surfaced. "He was killed two years after I moved into the flat. A suicide bomber. No one in his unit survived." He bowed his head and scooped a batch of samosas from the hot oil, tossing them onto a tray with unsteady hands.

Nancy's eyes held a warmth he had come to know well. "I'm sorry, Amitbhai. I know how hard it is for you to talk about this. I shouldn't keep pressing you for more stories."

He shook his head and steadied himself against the counter. "But, memsahib, if I don't tell you, who else will I tell?"

For the next few days, he noticed, Nancy didn't ask for any more stories. He listened while she told him about the latest arguments with her parents, who kept trying to arrange a marriage for her even though they despaired of finding a suitable match at her age. She talked about what she would do once she finished her novel—she had already been in touch with prospective publishers. He hoped she wouldn't be too disappointed if nobody wanted to read it.

One evening, as Amit was emptying a bucket of soapy water onto the sand behind the stall, a man in a khaki uniform approached him, bearing a thick brown envelope. He told Amit he was from the BMC and had come to serve Amit notice that his food stall did not comply with the Special Commission guidelines.

"What is this Special Commission?" Amit asked.

The man shoved the envelope at Amit. "Read it. Everything is explained in the notice." He turned away with a stiff, awkward movement.

Amit's pulse began to race as he sifted through several pages of writing in Marathi, a language that he read with some difficulty in spite of his many years in Bombay. Affixed to the documents with a large, gleaming paper clip was a sheet that contained several drawings and measurements.

"Arrey, Subash!" Subash would be able to read it, he knew. "Subash," he called again, his voice rising in pitch.

"Calm down, old man." Subash walked over to the counter, wiping his damp hands on his trousers. "What's the matter? Is your vada pav on fire?"

Amit gave him the papers, watching his face closely while he read them. A frown grew on Subash's broad forehead. He translated several portions of the notice into Hindi. The Special Commission had been appointed by the municipal commissioner to oversee the beautification of Girgaum Chowpatty. It had determined that Amit's food stall did not meet specifications. He had thirty days to rebuild it. If he failed to comply, the stall would be demolished, and he would lose his license.

Amit leaned on his crutch. "What should I do, Subash?"

"There's not much you can do, old man." Subash's eyes held a glimmer of sympathy as he handed the papers back to Amit. "They're trying to make a clean sweep of this place. Rebuild it into something more organized—they call it Bhel Plaza. My friend Ramdas, who runs a nariyal pani stall further up the beach, received a similar notice yesterday. And I've heard of more."

"Do you think they want a bribe?" Amit stuffed the papers back into the envelope, holding it by one corner as if it would burst into flames at any moment.

Subash shrugged. "They always want bribes. Whether it will stop them, I don't know."

That night, Amit resolved to tally his month's earnings and expenses, keeping aside money for the rent. From what was left, together with his savings, he would have enough for a handsome bribe. Surely it would be the only way to avoid seeing his stall demolished. He knew it would be far less than the money he needed to rebuild.

He explained this line of reasoning to Nancy the next day, but her reaction surprised him. Just do what they want, she told him. Yes, it would cost more, but at least he would be in compliance with their orders, and they wouldn't harass him again. He shook his head, amused by her innocence. She was young, he said, and didn't know how things worked in the city, even though she'd lived there all her life.

He stuffed the money in a grimy envelope and buried it in a sack of potatoes under the counter. A few days later, he saw the man in the khaki uniform again and hailed him. He explained that he did not have the funds necessary to rebuild the stall, but he was sure they could come to an understanding. He handed the fat envelope to the official, who took it without a word, slipping it into his briefcase as he walked away.

The deadline passed without incident, and Amit congratulated himself on the success of his plan. A week later, the same BMC official returned with another envelope, decorated with a bright red wax seal on the flap. "This is your final notice," he told Amit. "You have two weeks to comply with the Special Commission's order."

Amit's stomach churned. He clasped the official's hands and pleaded for more time. The man listened in stony silence, brushing Amit's hands away. He told him he would give him three weeks but not a day more.

"How are you going to raise the money?" Nancy asked when he told her about the extension. He hadn't said a word to her about the bribe, careful not to reveal how desperate his financial situation had become.

"Don't worry, memsahib," he said, trying to sound cheerful. "I have some savings, and I can get a loan from Lalwani sahib. I am sure he will help me out after I explain the matter."

Nancy pursed her lips and her eyes searched his face. For a moment, he feared she could see right through his deception. Then she offered to lend him some money herself. He refused at once, horrified by the thought. "But why?" she said. "Why won't you let me help you?"

Amit hung his head. He didn't want to tell her he was so ashamed of what he'd done, and that he should have listened to her all along. He reassured her that Mr. Lalwani would help him. If he didn't, then Amit would accept her offer. That seemed to satisfy her, and she left without asking him any questions.

In the end, Mr. Lalwani lent him the money, refusing to collect interest and offering him generous payment terms. On the advice of a few other vendors going through the same ordeal, Amit hired a contractor familiar with the situation.

"I wouldn't even think of visiting another food stall, Amitbhai," Nancy said, when he told her he would be rebuilding and offered to make arrangements with a nearby vendor. He reminded her that it was only for a few days, that he would be up and running again soon. With a week to go before the BMC deadline, he was confident everything would be ready in time.

True to his word, the contractor arrived at sunrise with two other men who began to tear down the stall. Amit had already cleared out his supplies the day before, and the men worked through the morning without a break. They disappeared at lunch time. Amit sat on an overturned crate facing the ocean and watched the waves rolling in, hoping the new stall would be the end of his troubles. Not only his—at least a dozen other vendors were busy working on their own stalls. After a while, Amit walked around the beach, stopping to chat with a few old acquaintances who had already rebuilt their stalls. The vendors assured him they were now in full compliance with the BMC order, pending final approval by the inspector who would be visiting the following week.

When the workers didn't return that afternoon, Amit grew increasingly worried. "Relax, old man," Subash said. "They are doing several jobs around here. They will be back—if not today, tomorrow." After an hour, Amit decided to go home. There was no point sitting there in the blistering sun without anything to do.

In spite of the slow start, Amit was relieved to see the workers return a day before the deadline. They finished the demolition, and the new stall began to take shape. While they were busy that evening, Nancy came by to review their progress. Amit hopped up from his crate, his eyes sparkling with excitement. Nancy laughed at him, telling him she hoped he wouldn't raise his prices too much now that he was going to have a brand new stall. In all honesty, the thought had never entered Amit's mind. All the same, he vowed his prices would stay exactly as they were.

When the contractor declared the work complete, Amit hovered around the stall, as Subash watched with a bemused smile. At last he had the place to himself once more. He inspected every square centimeter of it, delighting in the syrupy odor of fresh paint, marveling at the shining new stainless steel countertop (the old one had been a rough-hewn piece of wood), checking all the storage areas, and exclaiming at the efficiency of the new space arrangement.

Subash helped him load all his supplies and showed him how the gas-fired stove worked. Amit rubbed his hands together as he looked at the crisp, stenciled letters on the sign above the stall: "Jai Jawan Eatables and Drinks." His chest swelled with pride. Definitely, this new stall would be good for business. Maybe he could even pay off Mr. Lalwani's loan early. For the first time in days, his phantom leg stopped itching.

The news rippled throughout the community in minutes. The BMC inspector was making his rounds, scribbling in a leather-bound notebook as he examined each rebuilt stall. Amit sat behind his counter, wringing his hands with impatience, barely able to serve the few customers who stopped by to congratulate him on the upgrade. At last, he spotted the familiar khaki uniform.

Unlike the previous official, the inspector was a thin man, shorter than Amit, with a wispy mustache, paan-stained lips, and a gleaming bald spot. He told Amit to wait outside, then began fussing with a metal tape measure, checking the length of the counter and the height of the poles that held the sign aloft. He spent a great deal of time fiddling with the gas stove, muttering to himself and writing in his notebook at every turn. He washed his hands in the tiny sink at the back of the stall, then peered under it to check the drainage system and the holding tank. Amit leaned on his crutch, watching the inspector's every move. After almost an hour, the inspector put his notebook away and stuck his pen behind one ear. He told Amit he would receive a report in a week and left, still carrying on his one-sided conversation.

Two weeks passed before Amit received a visit from the first BMC official. He bore an envelope once again, with a wax seal on the flap. He handed it to Amit and consulted a typewritten list in his hand.

"Your stall does not comply with BMC specifications as set forth by the Special Commission," he said, checking off an entry on his list with a blue pen. "You have three weeks to meet these specifications," he gestured to the envelope, "failing which your stall will be demolished."

Amit stumbled forward, resting his hands on the counter to steady himself. A muffled roaring sounded in his ears above the murmur of the waves, and a sharp pain pierced his chest.

"But I don't understand," he said, as his chest heaved. "I have already rebuilt this stall according to the BMC specifications. There must be some mistake."

The official shrugged. "You can take it up with the Special Commission. If you wish to challenge this decision, you must file your case in court before the deadline."

Amit felt the crutch slipping away from beneath his arm. His knees buckled as the world spun around him, and he collapsed into an untidy heap on the sand.

*

Amit stood by Subash's stall, watching as a group of men swung their hammers and pick-axes. Nancy waited with him. She had taken the day off work so she could help him pack. The three of them waited in silence as the sign toppled and fell. Soon, the rest of the stall's framework lay in splintered piles. The men began carrying away larger pieces of the counter, grumbling and swearing under their breath. A BMC supervisor, smoking a bidi, barked instructions. Two hours later, nothing remained except a few scraps that lay, like bright blue pockmarks, on the sand.

Nancy held Amit's arm as they walked back to his flat. He had already collected his belongings in the middle of the living room, and she helped him arrange them in a frayed suitcase—a gift from Mr. Lalwani. Nancy looked around, checking to see if he had left anything behind.

"Are you sure you want to do this, Amitbhai?" He noticed how unsteady her voice was and hoped she wouldn't start crying.

He nodded. "When I arrived here, this city was called Bombay. Although I will never forget what happened during the war, I still had a dream, like many who come here. I was ready for a new life, a new home.

"Now it is Mumbai, and the dream is over. When I return to my village, at least I will have some peace and quiet. And I will find old friends there who will welcome me and invite me into their homes. I will visit places I have known since I was a boy, and I will not have to worry about dealing with the BMC anymore. It will be a new life for the second time."

Nancy said nothing but squatted on the floor across from him. He saw her lower lip quiver, but her eyes remained dry.

All at once, a deep, gut-wrenching sadness engulfed him. He wondered if she would ever finish her book now.

He gazed at her small, round face, imprinting it in his memory. "Nancy memsahib?"

"Yes, Amitbhai?"

"Would you like to hear one more story? About how I lost my leg?"

She stared at him for a moment, her face betraying no expression. Then, slowly, she nodded. As he began to speak, he saw that she did not turn on her tape recorder.

Glossary

aam papad: fruit leather made of sun-dried mango pulp

arrey: exclamation, equivalent to "hey!"

attar: fragrant essential oil, typically produced from flowers

ayah: female domestic servant, often employed as a nanny or nursemaid

balchao: spicy pickle cooked in a tomato-based sauce; usually made from shrimp or pork

batch: graduating class

bebinca: traditional Goan dessert flavored with coconut and baked in layers

bidi: thin, hand-rolled cigarette

biscuit: cookie

chawl: tenement buildings with single-room dwellings and common balconies and bathrooms; often built around a central courtyard or open area

chikki: sweet made from unrefined cane sugar and nuts, similar to peanut brittle

chivda: spicy snack food made from a variety of ingredients, usually including puffed rice and twigs of chickpea flour

choli: tight-fitting cropped blouse worn under a sari

dhansakh: traditional slow-cooked Parsi dish made from rice, lentils, vegetables, and mutton; generally prepared on Sundays

dhoti: men's garment, usually made of thin cotton fabric, wrapped around the waist like a loincloth

double-E: electrical engineering

dupatta: long scarf worn with both the salwar kameez and the kurta pajama

feni: popular Goan distilled liquor made from cashew fruit or coconut

flat: apartment or condominium in a multi-dwelling building

Goan: native of the Indian state of Goa (formerly a Portuguese colony); more broadly used to describe anyone with connections to or roots in Goa

golawala: vendor of flavored ice

goonda: ruffian, thug

jari puranawala: vendor who purchases used household items like bottles, cans, and newspapers for recycling or resale

khichri: rice and lentils cooked together

kukri: knife with a curved blade of Nepalese origin, traditionally used by Gurkha regiments in the army

kurta: loose-fitting, long-sleeved shirt without a collar

lathi: wooden stick or cane used as a weapon by police

lift: elevator

maalishwala: male practitioner of massage, typically for the head, neck, and shoulders

makapao: slang term for a Goan; more broadly, any Christian

mandap: outdoor hall or porch used for Hindu religious ceremonies

mosambi: sweet lime

mussalmaan: Muslim; derived from Urdu and Farsi languages

paan: preparations of areca nut, tobacco, and other ingredients wrapped in a betel leaf

panchayat: local governing body or council

parijata: long-lived flowering tree revered in Hindu mythology

pavement: sidewalk

puri bhaji: cooked vegetables, usually containing potatoes and greens (bhaji) served with deep-fried bread (puri)

Rexine: trademark for a synthetic leather product manufactured in England; used more generally to describe any synthetic leather product used in upholstery

sali murghi: spicy chicken served with thinly sliced strips of fried potatoes

salwar kameez: loose trousers with narrow ankles (salwar), worn with a long-sleeved shirt (kameez)

samosa: deep-fried pastry filled with spiced potatoes, vegetables, or ground meat; served with a selection of chutneys

sorpotel: traditional Goan dish of Portuguese origin containing boiled meat, usually pork, cooked in a spicy sauce flavored with vinegar

standard: grade in school; the Indian primary and secondary education system comprises kindergarten through the tenth standard

supari: mixture of crushed areca nut and spices sold in pouches; used as a digestive aid and breath freshener

tendli: ivy gourd, tindora
thermocol: styrofoam or expanded polystyrene
tiffin: lunch
torch: flashlight
vada pav: deep-fried potato fritter sandwich

Acknowledgements

Many have contributed, directly or indirectly, to bringing this book to fruition. In particular, I'd like to thank:

Paul Dyer, for beta reading and innumerable discussions, literary and otherwise.

Pam and Mark Coelho, for beta reading.

Kari Held, for beta reading and expert graphic design advice.

Yesenia Vargas, for meticulous copyediting and proofreading services.

The South Central Wisconsin Library System; especially the Fitchburg Public Library, where most of this book was written and edited.

The Madison NaNoWriMo community.

The global village of independent authors on Facebook, Twitter, LinkedIn, and the Absolute Write Water Cooler: we are not alone, indeed.

And finally, my wife and early beta reader, Donna; my daughter, Maya; and my dog, Chance. They tolerated my frequent disappearances into my writing cave without complaint and only a few barks of annoyance.